Notable published works by Maia Wojciechowska

A KINGDOM
IN A HORSE

A KINGDOM
IN A HORSE

Maia Wojciechowska

Sky Pony Press • New York

Sky Pony Press books may be purchased in bulk at special discounts for sales promotion, corporate gifts, fund-raising, or educational purposes. Special editions can also be created to specifications. For details, contact the Special Sales Department, Sky Pony Press, 307 West 36th Street, 11th Floor, New York, NY 10018 or info@skyhorsepublishing.com.

Sky Pony® is a registered trademark of Skyhorse Publishing, Inc.®, a Delaware corporation.

Visit our website at www.skyponypress.com.

10 9 8 7 6 5 4 3 2 1

Manufactured in Canada, October 2011
This product conforms to CPSIA 2008

Library of Congress Cataloging-in-Publication Data is available on file.

ISBN: 978-1-61608-481-3

for Elsie McCoy
and Oriana's horse

A KINGDOM
IN A HORSE

Chapter One

What he liked most about traveling by train was the feeling of drowsiness that seemed to be part of the clattering of wheels against the tracks. Trains were made for daydreaming, he decided, and then smiled to himself. His father and the other rodeo men were not daydreaming; they were asleep, their long legs extended between the seats, their hats pulled down over their faces, their thumbs in the buckled belts of their jeans. It's funny, he thought, how very alike they are, and how like them I have become.

There was a time when he was not like them at all. There was a time when he was hardly aware that he had a father and that his father was Lee Earl. He lived with his mother then, and he would hide behind her when the thin stranger with a scar running the length of his face would come to visit them. His mother would tell him that this man was his father and that his father was a very famous all-around cowboy. But that knowledge did nothing to the boy; the man frightened him, and he was glad whenever he went away.

He was only five when his mother died and the stranger he feared became the one and only person he now had. And as suddenly as his whole life had collapsed for him, a new existence began. His father became his whole world. He began to travel the rodeo circuit with him.

"I want to make people laugh and the riders safe," his father said when he explained to him his decision to become a rodeo clown. "And besides, being a clown will give me more time to be with you."

And now he was David Earl, Lee's son, and that was something to be proud of, for Lee Earl was no ordinary clown. He was the greatest rodeo clown in the world. Lee Earl was a champion clown, the best, the smartest, the funniest, and the most imaginative and daring rodeo clown who ever lived. That's what everyone said, and that's what they wrote about him in newspapers and magazines.

The fact that his father was the very best made up for many things—things like not having friends his own age, no school to go to, and no home besides a series of dingy hotel rooms. It even made up for not having a mother.

"When you're thirteen," his father used to say to him, "I'll let you come in with me. You'll be the barrel man and I'll be the infighter."

"Why can't I start now?" the boy would ask. He knew the answer but hoped, each time they talked about it, that his father might change his mind.

"Thirteen is early enough," his father would say. "At thirteen you'll be man enough for the job. Besides . . ."

Besides, thirteen was Lee Earl's lucky number.

Waiting for that birthday was like waiting for snow in the Texas panhandle. But while waiting, he was happy because he loved everything about his life. He loved the traveling, the excitement of crisscrossing the wide expanse of the West and Southwest. He was part of the "suicide" circuit, part of men who have chosen gambling with their very lives. He loved the long evenings of sitting around with the rodeo riders, listening to them. They lied too much, smoked too much, drank too much, and were too quick of temper, but it was from them that he learned the reason why he, David Earl, would have no other life but the rodeo life.

The stories they told of the great riders and their horses, of the memorable events they had witnessed or heard about, made the natural boundaries for that life. And within the confines of those boundaries he meant to live. Always. He and his father.

While waiting for his thirteenth birthday, David was learning. He was learning how to be a rodeo clown. No one ever had to tell him what it was that the clown did. He saw that for himself. The clown was there not only to get laughs, he was there to divert the Brahman bull's attention from a thrown rider. That was the important part, the part that was pure danger. For no man can outrun a bull bent on killing. The timing was the thing. Without timing there would be no live clowns, only dead ones.

He learned most from watching his father. While the crowd saw a ludicrous figure in an outlandish costume—a bald-headed skullcap with a red fringe on his head, exaggerated makeup on his face—gawking at a thundering ton of bull flesh with lowered horns, the boy would watch his father's feet; he would judge the distance, he would measure the speed of the turns, the bull's and his father's. He knew that behind the makeup his father's face was as tense as that of any man risking death. He knew that his father's brain became a machine, working with the accuracy of a watch. And while the crowd was in stitches at the clowning of the man who made the death ballet seem like slapstick, the boy saw that his father was saving the riders' lives and, in exchange, risking his own.

There had been many famous clowns before Lee Earl, and David knew what made them famous, but now his father was said to be better than any of them. Like them, he was tough and he was smart. And when he was hurt he would not show it. When one of his bones would break under the impact of an encounter with a Brahman, he would not tell anyone, not even his son. That was why the boy would watch his father sleep. If he saw him wince in his dreams, he would know that the hurt was not a minor one. He would have a doctor come in to examine his father in the hotel room early in the morning when he could not protest.

But clowning was not everything to the boy. Like his father, he intended to make his name in other standard events, the saddle-bronc riding, the calf roping, bareback riding, steer wrestling, and Brahman bull riding.

He knew as much about the horses that made the history of rodeo as he did about the men. The greatest of the "critters" was Midnight, the most magnificent bucker of the 1932–36 rodeos. He threw the best of the riders, and when he died, a cortege of three hundred men whose bones he had managed to break mourned at his funeral. And he knew about other horses who had a sudden and unending hatred of the saddle: War Paint, Miss Klamath, Yellow Fever, and Five Minutes to Midnight.

But his special love was reserved for the horses that were friends rather than enemies of man. The American quarter horse, like its master, came out of a brutal struggle for the survival of the fittest, and it had to be lithe, fast, and intelligent to win that struggle.

As the train rushed through majestically beautiful but desolate Wyoming, David was thinking of the horse that he would buy for himself. On his thirteenth birthday he would become a clown. That day, only eight months away, would be the day he would begin to save for that horse. He did not even want to look around for one before he could afford to buy it. He could wait. The kind of horse he would buy was the kind he would know he wanted the minute he saw it.

He had it all figured out—how he was going to board his horse, ship it from place to place, when he was going to ride it, and what he was going to teach it. He would, like his father, be a rodeo clown, but he also wanted to become a champion roper. And for that to happen he had to own a horse that was smarter than himself. A horse like Baldy. He had heard the old-timers talk of Baldy, and he knew that that horse could do anything but tie a knot. And that's the kind of horse he was going to get for himself.

The signs were all over the small Wyoming town. Nearly ten thousand people had come for the annual rodeo, some having driven as far as eight hundred miles to see his father, the rodeo's main attraction.

**LEE EARL
THE CLOWN**

with 2 bulls
and 2 men
coming out at the
SAME TIME

David was awakened, like so many times before, by the staccato beat of hoofs echoing from the buildings and the macadam pavement of the main street. He jumped out of bed to watch the horses pass under his hotel window. Each time he saw the parade of rodeo horses his throat would tighten. Soon he would be riding his own horse to the arena.

There was a dust storm that day out in the plains beyond the town, and the gray-yellow of the blowing sand seemed to encircle the town in a sort of a prison. His father was putting on makeup that would make his face like a mask, unrecognizable; and David suddenly felt an impulse to tell him about the horse he intended to buy. There was something about the dust storm, and his father's whitening face, that made him want to share this secret with his father. But he decided against it. He too was superstitious. He did not want to endanger the dream by talking about it.

David was standing at the rails, alone as was his habit, not talking to anyone, when the bull riding started. Most rodeos limit a man to one bull ride, and only one bull is released at a time. To have two bulls and two riders come out at the same time was even more dangerous than the Texas "mad scrambles," during which ten riders, ten bulls, and ten clowns are turned out at the same time. But David knew that his father was not worried. This was August 13, and thirteen was Lee's lucky number. The two riders would not worry even if it were not the thirteenth. "With Lee Earl as the rescue man," the saying went, "you're as safe as in your own bed."

The bellowing bulls could be heard long before they came out of the chutes. They emerged, two of them, big and mean, with riders seated precariously on their huge backs. Each rider held the unbuckled rope with one hand, using the other for balance against the bull's high kicks. Within what seemed a split second, the bulls collided one against the other. Lee had torn off his skullcap and held it as a lure in his left hand, while with his right he waved the dunce cap. At the moment of the collision he was so close to the animals that their impact sent him sprawling.

Even before the people began to laugh at the sight of the clown in the dust, David knew that this was not part of the act, that his father did not mean to fall. He had vaulted the railing and was running toward his father who was already on his feet.

"Get back!" Lee shouted to David.

But at that instant both riders were unseated. It happened so very fast that no one could later tell for sure whether the riders were midway coming down or still going up. Lee was caught, not by one animal but by both simultaneously. A horn of each bull tore into him and he was not tossed; rather he seemed to be ripped apart as the bulls separated with pieces of his clothing on their horns.

David was on his knees at his father's side when two shots rang out, and the two bulls were down and dead within seconds of their angry exit from the chutes.

The arena filled instantly with people. Someone was pulling at David's arms and he did not know whether he was being lifted or carried, but he struggled against the hands that held him, wanting to see, to reach his father. Tears obscured his vision and his own angry shouts of "Let me go!" were loud in his ears.

In the ambulance as he sat at his father's side he did not dare look at the white face below him but stared out of the rear window of the screaming vehicle at the dust storm moving closer to town.

"I wouldn't believe it if I weren't seeing it," the fat doctor said. David was just inside the door, not wanting to see what the blood was hiding. "The horns hit the hip bones on both sides and seemed to have bounced back."

An intern and a nurse were bending down over his father, and the doctor kept pointing his fat finger.

"About fifteen inches of flesh torn clear from the bone!"—he gave a low whistle—"on both sides! And the bones are just fine. All we need to do is clean the wounds and stitch the flesh back together."

And that was that. A miracle, some said. David thought it had more to do with that day being the thirteenth of the month.

Within three hours he was permitted to go into the room and talk to his father.

"How do you feel?" he asked.

"As if someone had tickled me," his father said and tried to laugh. David knew the pain was bad, in spite of everything the doctor said. He had seen that look of pain before. But this time there was something new in his father's eyes, a light he had never seen there.

"They say you'll be all right," David said.

"You and I. Both of us will be all right," his father said.

And with that he turned his face to the wall. It was not until the next day that David understood what his father meant.

"As soon as they let me get up," his father told him, "we're taking off for Vermont."

"Vermont?" That was the end of the world. Up north, in the east, where there are no horses, no rodeos, nothing.

"Your mother came from there," his father was

saying. "Once I promised her a house. I've been paying for one ever since you were born. I didn't tell her about it because I wanted it to be a surprise. And now it's ours."

"What for? What do we need with a house?" David said, shivering. He had never before felt a premonition of disaster. Now he felt it in the unfamiliar weakness in his knees, in the tightness of his throat, and in that strange light in his father's eyes.

"We'll live in that house," his father said.

"But why? Why would we want to live in a house, in Vermont?" he shouted angrily.

"Because—" his father began softly, but then his voice rose also in anger—"because I don't want us to end up like the rest in some forsaken grave!"

It couldn't be, the boy thought, it couldn't be that his father had forgotten all about his promise. His father reached his hand to touch him, but David moved away from the bed.

"When I first started to pay for this house," his father said quietly, not looking at his son but toward the open window, "I was only thinking of your mother. But this last year I often thought that the two of us ought to belong somewhere. Normal people don't live like we do. They greet each other on the streets by name. They walk into a store, and the owner knows what they came to buy. It's a fine kind of life and you'll love it—"

"I'd hate it!"

"You've got to understand," his father said firmly, "everything's changed now. I'll never go back into that arena. Never again."

David ran out of the hospital, away from his father's words, away from that light in his eyes, away from the sickeningly sweet smell of that room. The town was quiet now, with the rodeo gone and the dust settled somewhere else. He sat on a log, for hours, until darkness came, trying to figure things out. At first he thought that his father had turned into a coward, but he dismissed that thought. Why, then? All he knew was that his father had broken his promise to him. He had waited until he was almost thirteen to tell him that the waiting was for nothing. His life now was finished. There was to be no future for him. And what he had to learn now was to forget the past.

Chapter Two

He hated everything—the town, the house, the school, the children, Vermont, and most of all he hated his father. In the first month he tried running away twice. He was going to go west, join a rodeo on his own; he would change his name and become a bronco rider, the best who ever lived. He would get himself a horse that would make old Baldy look like a donkey. There would be nothing in his life except that horse of his, no friends, no family, no memories. No one would be able to hurt him because he would never trust anyone; he would never count on anyone. A horse could not cheat you out of a dream; a horse would never lie to you.

Both attempts at running away ended in failure. The

first time he hitchhiked a ride. The truck driver seemed to him like a trustworthy sort of a man, and he told him his last name and almost confided to him that he had run away. They stopped for breakfast, and the driver must have called Lee. Within half an hour David was back home. What was so humiliating about that attempt was the fact that until the truck driver called, his father was unaware of David's disappearance.

The very next week David bought a second-hand bicycle with some money he had and tried running away again. This time his father caught up with him before night fell. And once again David felt humiliated. He was hungry and cold and pitying himself when his father found him.

"I don't want you to try running away again," his father said on the way back. "I tried to make you understand why it is that I had to quit the rodeo. It would never have worked for us." He paused and put an arm around David's shoulders. "That was a dumb promise I made you. One day you'll forgive me because you'll understand that sometimes dreams have to end. I had a dream too, us, working together. It ended the second I saw you inside the arena."

The explanation didn't mean anything to David. He grew more bitter after that. He decided to wait until he was sixteen and then leave. Openly, not sneaking away. Whatever would happen to him between now and then wouldn't matter. At sixteen he would begin to live again.

But again time seemed to stand still. The day of his thirteenth birthday came, and he tried not to think about the past or what this day was once to mean to him. He was glad his father had forgotten it was his birthday.

"I'd like you to drive with me to Burlington this evening," his father said after dinner that day.

"Do I have to? I've got homework to do," David said, getting up from the table.

"I thought you'd finished it. I saw you shut the last book, and you sighed."

"I was going to study ahead for the test," David said impatiently.

"I need you to come with me. Get your coat."

Since they moved to Vermont his father had worked at all sorts of odd jobs, but blacksmithing was the thing that he did well, often, and enjoyed most. David would go with him whenever he had difficult horses to shoe or so many that his help was needed.

They had pulled up in front of the complex of buildings where the monthly horse auction took place. When his father got out of the truck without taking his tools with him, David suddenly realized that his father had not forgotten his birthday, and that they had come here to look for a horse. He felt tricked and angry.

"I don't know if I ever told you," David said coldly to his father as they walked through the parking lot already beginning to fill up with cars, "but I really hate horses. I wouldn't have one for a million dollars."

He watched his father's face as he said it, and by the dim light he saw it change. The look of pain came over it, and he turned his eyes away.

"That couldn't be true," his father said calmly. "You've always loved horses."

"I used to love a lot of things," David said, and once again he looked up at his father.

His father's eyes blinked and then hardened. They walked silently, side by side, each feeling himself a stranger to the other.

David did not mean to look at the horses, and he stayed back at the entrance of the great barn as his father walked the length of it looking over the animals. What caught David's attention was a chestnut mare which stood in the passageway between the stalls. She was held by a man with a cane. There was nothing particularly special about her; she did not look well cared for, and her limpid blue eye, "the watch eye," was not that unusual in a western horse. She has as much quarter horse in her, he thought, as she has thoroughbred. Her conformation was good, her legs strong, yet as thin and long as a race horse's. Her neck would look better if the mane were either cut shorter or let grow. Whoever had cut the mane had done an equally bad job on the tail. It fell less than half way to the ground. The mare's hips were outlined, the bones pressing against the dirty coat. He liked the wide white mark running from her eyes and narrowing slightly at the nostrils. And more than that, he liked the way the mare looked at him, with the soft brown eye and the very light blue one. It seemed to mock him, that look.

During his years with the rodeo David learned to ride and he learned about horses. There was a certain look among horses which he came to recognize as the look of the kind of horse he wanted for himself, the look of independence. He had argued several times about that particular look, with men who did not agree with him that it made for a good horse. On the contrary, most of the men insisted that a horse who looked self-reliant was an indifferent mount, one hard to control and difficult to teach. Yet he was always attracted by a horse whose expression seemed to say to him, "I don't need you." And the chestnut mare seemed to be saying exactly that to him.

David moved away from the mare, angry at himself for having been attracted to her. The stable was at least four hundred feet long, and he noticed his father still walking away from him.

"Hey, kid," a voice behind him said, and he turned around. The man with the cane was addressing him.

"If you're looking for a horse for yourself, this here mare's the best of the lot."

"I'm not looking for a horse," he said curtly and walked on. The stalls, about forty feet wide and deep, were filled with animals—full-grown saddle horses and ponies. Beautifully groomed ones were standing next to others that looked pitifully thin, more dead than alive. There were many hack horses, old slaves that were going to be bought by riding stables and summer camps, who had spent all of their lives shuttled between incompetent riders and cruel masters.

If I were rich, David thought suddenly, I'd have a place just for old hack horses. A big pasture and a good dry barn where they would live, never ridden, until they died from old age.

He looked away from one horse with a wide gash in its forehead from which fresh blood was flowing to join the rivulets of dried blood that reached its forelegs. He had been to many horse auctions, and he was always made furious by the sight of an animal that had been hurt in an overloaded trailer.

Making his way back through the passageway, now filled with people, he saw his father talking to the man with the cane. He wanted that mare more than anything he ever wanted in his life, even more than he wanted to be a rodeo clown. He could go up to his father now, apologize for what he had said about not wanting a horse. He could tell him that he'd pay him back if he were to buy that horse for him. He could even act like a kid and beg. This was his chance! His father was now petting the mare's neck and looking down at her feet.

David bit his lower lip. He could do none of those things. He could not ask his father to forgive him, nor could he ask for the horse. If he did ask, and if he were given the horse he would once again feel chained to his father. By love and gratitude. A double burden. And he had learned how to do without burdens. He had learned how to live alone. He turned his back and walked away to the exit door.

The enclosure of the auction hall was packed by the time they reached the tiers of wooden seats. The seats formed a horseshoe above the auctioneer's high desk and the sawdust floor. The tack was being sold from station wagons parked where the horses later on would be shown. They found seats in the highest tier and David sat a few feet away from his father, leaving a space in between, hoping that someone would separate them. No sooner had they sat down than an old lady did sit down between his father and him. He looked at her sideways, wondering what she could possibly be doing in this place filled with horse traders, camp owners and horse breeders. In her tweed suit she seemed very much out of place among the blue jeans and sport shirts which were worn even by the few women present.

"Could you help me?" David heard her whisper to his father.

"Sure, ma'am. What can I do for you?" his father answered immediately.

"I would like to buy something for a horse," the old woman said, and David, glancing at her profile, noticed that she had blushed. "But I don't seem to understand what is being sold and how to bid."

"What would you like to buy?" Lee asked.

"Well . . ." she hesitated. "Everything that a horse might need."

"What kind of a horse do you have?"

"I haven't got one. Not yet. That's why I'm here. To buy one."

"You're sure putting the cart before the horse." They both laughed at that, and David turned his face away from them and toward the auction floor.

"Are you looking for a western or an English horse?" Lee asked.

"I don't know," she whispered, and after a moment added, "I'm afraid I wouldn't know the difference."

David shifted in his seat, and the woman turned toward him and smiled. He did not return the smile but instead looked directly in front of him at a man who was reading a newspaper. What would an old woman want with a horse? he wondered angrily.

"Who are you buying the horse for?" his father asked, and he heard the woman catch her breath.

David waited for her to answer, and when she finally did, her voice seemed louder than she had intended it to be.

"For myself."

It was funny, David thought, but in a way that could not be laughed at. Her brave admission was a fine thing, the sort of thing adults rarely did. She could have lied.

"Then," his father was saying, "I think I know the horse for you. I saw it a few minutes ago. It looked very gentle, and it's a mare, not young, mind you, but she's still got a lot of life in her. The man who was selling her said that she rides both English and western. I'd say you should get yourself a western saddle. They're much more comfortable to ride in, and you can always get an English one later on."

He was telling her about the chestnut mare! Ever since he had seen her, David had hoped desperately that something would happen, that something might be said, by his father or by him. He wanted that horse! It was exactly the kind of horse that he had always hoped he would meet and own. That horse alone would change his whole life. If he only had it, nothing would matter. He could go on living in Vermont forever. His school, the house, his father, he could no longer hate anything, he would no longer have time to hate. But his thoughts suddenly filled him with an angry sadness. He was mad at himself for wanting that animal so much, mad for being ready to be "bought" back into living happily. And he was sad because they were now talking about getting a used saddle and all the other things the mare would need. And he knew it was too late for wishing. The old woman and not he would have the mare.

"If you want," his father was saying to the woman, "I'll bid on the tack for you. I know a good buy when I see it. Although from up here it would be hard to tell. We should go down and stand by the auctioneer, and we could examine the things we buy."

"Oh, could we do that?"

"Sure," Lee said and leaned across the woman. "David, let's go down."

He did not look up at his father.

"I'd rather stay here," he said.

"We'll need you," his father said with firmness, and David got up and followed them out.

"By the way," his father said and extended his hand to the woman, "my name's Lee Earl and that's my son, David."

"I'm Sarah Tierney," she said, shaking his father's hand. "Hello, David." But he had already passed them and pretended not to have heard.

"This is a sort of busman's holiday for me," Lee said quickly as if to distract the woman from David's impoliteness. "I do blacksmithing around Middlebury."

"Middlebury!" the woman cried happily. "It's not far from where I live. I have a farm near Cornwall."

"If you buy a horse then I'll probably be shoeing it. There's no one closer to you that I know of."

"That's marvelous!"

They had reached the auction floor. "*Abraduble-room!*" The auctioneer's voice was loud, yet his face did not show the strain of all the shouting he had to do. Lee had moved closer to the men who were standing around the auctioneer's raised desk. He was flipping over some used saddles and testing the leather on the bridles, and talking to those who were selling.

The woman turned toward David.

"Can you make out the words of the auctioneer?" she asked him.

"Sometimes," he answered, not looking at her or at anything in particular. He felt more miserable now than ever.

"Sold to Lee Earl!" the auctioneer shouted, and to David's and the woman's surprise a portion of the crowd applauded, some calling out his name.

"Your father must be someone famous," the woman said.

"He used to be in rodeos," David said sullenly.

"Oh," she said.

Lee was coming toward them carrying a large saddle and over it a blanket and a bridle.

"I got you a very good buy," he said to the woman.

Wordlessly David reached for the saddle and threw it over his shoulder. "You see, this is a Navaho blanket," his father continued, speaking to the woman. "It's soft and strong. Feel it. Sure, it's used, but it will last a lifetime. And the bridle is in very good shape too."

When they reached the mare, David didn't want to look up at her. He kept his eyes on the ground, and yet he could not help seeing how wonderfully thin her legs were and how small the hoofs.

"This here's the best animal of the lot," the man with the cane was saying. He moved the horse around for the woman to see, and then suddenly, dropping his cane, he bent down and limped half bent under the horse's belly and to the other side of it. He was smiling a toothless grin as he came back the same way. "Gentle as a puppy," he said, lifting his cane. "You couldn't do that with another horse that's here."

"What's her name?" the woman wanted to know.

"I don't know her name," the man answered and spat some tobacco juice. "Lady, I only sell them. I don't live with them. A private party wanted me to sell this here mare and I forgot to ask for her name."

The mare turned her head and the woman saw the blue eye.

"Is she blind?" she asked.

"Nah," the man said, "that's what's called a 'watch

eye.' It's very prized out West because a horse with an eye like that will see real good in the dark." Suddenly the man touched David with his cane. "Hey, you! Jump up on her, from the rear if you can."

The half-challenge, half-order was so unexpected that he stepped back, and then, quickly, did as he was told. I want to try her out, he thought, as he landed on the mare's back, cushioning his weight with the palms of his hands and sliding onto the beat-up saddle.

He leaned for the reins; then barely touching them he neck-reined to the right, and the mare turned as sharply as he knew she would and sprung immediately into a canter. Although there were people in the passageway between the stalls, the horse ran as if she were in an open field, smoothly and fearlessly. Coming to the end of the barn, she turned left at the touch of the reins and David caught his breath at the speed of that turn. With hardly a command from him the mare came to a sharp stop a foot away from the woman. David gently pulled back on the reins, and the animal backed up immediately, going in a straight line as long as the reins were not loosened, and when they were, she walked slowly forward, lifting her feet high and tossing her neck.

David slipped off, gave the reins to the man, and approached his father.

"Can I go back to the truck now?" he asked.

"You don't want to see the auction?"

"I've got some books. I'd rather study now." He didn't look at his father nor at the woman.

"Okay," his father said, "I'll be around for another hour."

He walked away very fast, without saying goodbye to the woman, without looking at the horse; and when he reached the truck he sat for a long while with his eyes closed, holding back the tears. And then, noiselessly, he began to cry.

Chapter Three

They had loved each other for almost half a century. During all those years Sarah had not once thought of how it would be to live without her husband.

The morning after the funeral had seemed very quiet except for the noises of birds and the slight movement of the new foliage. It was still cool but the air was scented with spring and the sun was drying the muddy earth. Sarah stood on the porch of her farmhouse, which her father had built in the exact center of the rectangular property. The house was surrounded on one side by a grove of maple trees and on the other three sides by fields. When they had decided they could no longer farm the fields, they plowed them and planted grass. In the middle of the summer the grass stood high and green. In the fall it turned yellow from the goldenrod growing freely in it. Not far from the house and in the back of it, stood the large barn where they had once kept cows. It was freshly painted white, as was the fence that enclosed the pasture and the house itself.

Sarah began to walk toward a little hill, from the top of which she could see her land stretch until it reached the hills on three sides and the highway on the north side. Beyond that was the edge of a pine forest.

She had always considered this her total world. As a child she lived here with her parents and her older brother. Shortly after he was killed in the First World War her mother died. For a while there were only her father and she. At nineteen her life seemed to really begin, yet her world remained the same. She married Paul Tierney, and but for a brief honeymoon trip to New York City, they had always lived here. When her father died, he left the property to Paul, for he had grown to love him as much as if he were his own son. As Paul and Sarah had no children, their world remained within this rectangle. Beyond it lay a strange country Sarah only liked to visit, because her world's center was here, and its axis was Paul. Now without him it seemed to her that she was in a strange and unfamiliar place.

She walked slowly back toward the house. She stopped by a square structure with three round windows. From the outside it looked somewhat like a little chapel. Once it had been a stable but for years it had been used as a storage place.

Suddenly she remembered something that she had completely forgotten. Her brother, when he was fifteen and she only eight, had had a horse. It was a black stallion with a white spot on its forehead. She could still see the animal quite vividly, and just as vividly she remembered crying in this stable.

Why did I cry, she tried to recall, unbolting the Dutch door of the stable. A shaft of light illuminated the dusty interior. There were tables and chairs and old trunks and picture frames. She walked inside the box stall and was amazed to see that it looked as if it were ready for a horse. It even had some straw covering the wooden floor, and there was no smell of mustiness. The feeder was still hanging in the corner.

She looked up toward one of the round windows with its network of shiny cobwebs. And now she remembered why it was that she had cried that day long ago. She had been forbidden by her brother even to come close to his horse and was told that she could never ride it. She had cried because she was jealous. She had cried because she wanted more than anything else to have a horse of her own.

She leaned against the gate of the stall. It would be

marvelous, she mused, to have a horse. The thought was so unexpected that she laughed. But it persisted, the crazy idea that she could now make a forgotten dream of her childhood come true. And why not? she reasoned with herself. Why not indeed? Paul would have thought it very sensible. It was as if he were present in the stable now, urging her to go ahead, not to hesitate. "You're one of the meek," he had once told her. "The world belongs to you and you don't even know it." Belonging. That was the most valid thing in life. Now she belonged to no one, and no living thing belonged to her.

I shall buy myself a horse, she decided.

With a light heart, humming to herself, Sarah walked around the stable, deciding which pieces of furniture she would give away, which she would burn, and which she would keep. "I'll keep this rocking chair," she said aloud, "and I'll keep it right here, so I can sit and watch my horse while it eats and rests."

She laughed suddenly. With the years, her laughter had become very much like her husband's.

Chapter Four

The night after the auction Sarah was too excited to sleep. Several times she laughed aloud at her happiness, and several times she felt strangely afraid of her deed.

"It is a crazy thing that I have done," Sarah muttered to herself, watching the big horse van coming up the winding dirt road.

Her back ached from the work she had been doing since early that morning. The stable was ready, clean and empty. She would have liked to have had time to paint it, but she would do that later. She had found enough salt hay to carpet the box stall a foot deep. There would be a lot of things she would have to do later, but she wasn't sure what they might be. She knew nothing of a horse's needs.

The red horse van disappeared in the spring foliage for a moment and then reappeared around the bend. Its redness moved among the leaves of the old maples that lined the road, and as it drew closer her heart began to pound faster. I'm scared of what I've done, she thought. She hoped that no one would see the horse van, for what would people say about a woman of sixty-four, living alone, who had gone off to the auction and bought herself a horse?

"Here we are," the man said. He got out of the high driver's seat with great difficulty and hobbled in one place for a moment. "To limber up my bum leg," he explained.

Sarah could hear the muffled sounds of a hoof scraping the floor of the van. She was most impatient to see her horse. The man got his cane and wanted to see the stable first.

"Once," he said, "I delivered a horse to a stable that wasn't fit for a pig. I always make it a practice to look first and then unload." Apparently he was satisfied with what he saw. "Sunny and dry," he said.

"You brought the hay and straw and the feed?" she asked.

"Yep. Brought all of it, enough to last you a month. Say, you wouldn't want to sell that mare, would you? After you left the auction, a young lady took a fancy to her and wanted to buy her. Wanted to pay two hundred for her. You'd make yourself thirty dollars."

"No, I wouldn't want to sell," she said firmly.

"She sure took a fancy to your mare," the man continued. "Funny thing, she insisted your horse wasn't yet nine. Anyone can see she's more than that, fifteen or sixteen, maybe. But it's a darn good horse you're getting. Who's going to ride her, your grandchildren?"

She didn't want him to know that she'd gotten the horse for herself.

"Couldn't we get her out?" she said, hoping he wouldn't repeat the question. "She must be very uncomfortable in that van."

"Are you kidding?" He laughed. "She's all alone in it. You should see how many horses this here van can hold. I can pack eighteen."

She remembered with a shudder having seen the horse with a gash in its forehead and Lee telling her about the unscrupulous horse traders who overpack the animals.

"I don't think she'll come down with shipping fever on you," the man was saying, "although you never know."

"What if she does? What should I do?" She was frightened by this.

"To tell you the honest truth I don't know how far she came from. If she came from out West, she might come down with the fever, but she certainly wouldn't have gotten it from just coming here from Burlington."

"But what should I do if she does get sick?" she

repeated, angry now at the man for talking so much and saying so little.

"You might get a vet or you might try to cure her yourself," the man said, spitting tobacco juice out of the side of his mouth.

"But how will I know that she is sick?"

"Oh, you'll know all right. Her nose and eyes will start running and she will cough a lot. It's sort of like pneumonia with people."

"Goodness," she whispered, terrified.

"You don't know much about horses, do you?" He didn't wait for an answer. "Thing is with horses, they can't breathe through their mouths, so it's important to keep their noses clean and free."

"But what should I do?" she asked once again, not angry but quite desperate.

"Keep her warm. You should make a hood out of a feed bag, get it over her head, and put a bucket underneath it with scalding hot water, bran tar, and Vick's VapoRub. Make her inhale it until her nose clears up. If that don't do the trick, then call the vet. There's one in Middlebury, Doc King. He'll give her a shot of penicillin." He spat the tobacco again and shifted his weight to his good foot. "As I said before, I don't know where she came from, or who brought her over. The good horse traders always give their horses inoculations along the way if they bring the animals from way off. If it was one of them cheap guys or a private party who don't know anything about transporting horses, she might come down with the fever on you."

How could I, Sarah thought, hold the horse's head in a feed bag, and how could I keep the water scalding hot? I will never be able to help her if she does get sick.

"But don't you start worrying before it's time. She didn't look to me as if she was coming down with anything." The man started walking to the van. He had frightened her so very much, and now he was giving her hope.

I won't worry, she decided, I won't worry at all. But she prayed all the same. Oh, don't let her get sick!

As the man was opening the door of the van she almost shouted to him to take the horse back, to sell it. Once again the feeling that she shouldn't have done it, that she shouldn't have bought the horse, intensified in her, now even more strongly than last night when she was driving back from the auction, because of the threat of the sickness. But she didn't cry out to the man. The horse, her horse, was coming down the plank.

The mare's ears quivered with excitement. Her eyes, the blue and the brown, were wide with expectation, and her whole body was tense. She walked down, shivering nervously, yet there was something regal in her. Maybe it was the head held high on the lovely long neck, maybe the steps—composed—or the expression on her face—haughty.

"She sure's got a lot of thoroughbred in her," the man said. "And lady, if you ever come across a more gentle horse than this one, just let me know."

He was holding on to her straw halter and leading her toward the stable while she looked all around her, moving her head from side to side. Sarah was walking slightly behind, yet the horse was watching her too, throwing side glances to see if she was still following.

"Most horses," the man was saying, "when they leave the van, if they let you get them off at all, act up and rear and get real nervous. Not this one! No siree! She walked into that van confident and she comes out like a queen surveying her new domain."

The man took the straw halter off when the horse was in the stall, looking for the hay that was not there.

"We better give her some hay. But don't feed her the oat mixture until tonight. She had some this morning."

"Do I just feed her twice a day?" Sarah asked.

"That's all, twelve hours apart. Like, let's say you feed her at seven in the morning, then don't feed her again until seven at night."

"How much of it should she have?" The man was still inside the stall, and the mare was still trying to find something to eat inside the salt hay. Then giving up, she raised her head and listened, her ears turning toward the person who spoke.

"I brought you an oat mixture that's got molasses and crushed corn in it. You give her about two quarts in the morning and two at night. Maybe a little more if she is going to get a lot of exercise."

"And the hay?"

"All she will eat. She needs to put on about two hundred pounds to get back in shape. The bales come in sections. Give her two, three sections at night when you bed her down, and maybe one or two in the pasture too, because the young grass don't have too much nourishment yet. You kept cows in that enclosed pasture, there, didn't you?"

"Yes," she said.

"Well, I better get your stuff in here. Say, you should get her some water. A bucket. She hasn't had any water, because of the trip."

Left alone with her horse, Sarah discovered to her great surprise that she was afraid. She was even too afraid to approach the animal. It looked so gigantic. She had not realized, when she was buying her, how large the mare was. And those eyes, the eyes that she had fallen in love with, were actually frightening now.

What will I do about this fear, she thought, and then, not wanting the horse to guess at her thoughts, she said aloud: "Last night when I couldn't sleep I was thinking of all sorts of names for you. I'd like to call you Gypsy. I don't know if you'll like it, it's rather plain, but I think it fits you." She looked hopelessly at the horse that was staring at her. "Oh, Gypsy, please don't get sick!"

"Where do you want it, lady?" the man was asking. On his back he carried a bale of hay—or was it straw?—she wondered.

"Oh, right here will be fine," she said, pointing to the closest spot to the stall.

The man laughed.

"If I leave this hay here the horse will help herself to it and scatter what she doesn't get at."

He took the bale to the farthest corner of the stable, kicking over the rocking chair Sarah had left in the corner. She picked it up and placed it next to where she had wanted the hay to go. When he left the stable, she spoke to the mare:

"I wouldn't mind it if you scattered the hay. I wouldn't mind it at all picking up after you. That's what I'm here for, to take care of you and to spoil you." She smiled at the animal, who was listening to her. "You see"—she pointed to the table where she had placed all the purchases she had made: the saddle, bridle, brush, and curry comb—"all of those things are yours. The only thing that is mine in here is the rocking chair."

She stopped speaking when the man came in with the second bale.

"I thought," he said sternly, "that you'd have given her some of this timothy by now. And water, you better get some."

She didn't say anything but blushed instead. She hated herself for this helplessness and ignorance as much as for the continuing fear she felt.

"That salt hay you've got for her bedding's no good. It's too expensive for one thing and won't make a good compost."

With a pitchfork he started pushing aside the hay she had so carefully placed in the stall and began to replace it with the yellow straw he had brought in.

He thinks that I can't do anything at all for Gypsy, she thought angrily, turning on her heels and walking to the well. She drew a bucket of water and carried it to the stable. The man was not inside; he had already given Gypsy a section of hay, and Sarah said to her, "I'll walk right in and put this bucket in the corner. Please don't do anything like kicking me."

The horse lifted its head from the hay at the sound of her voice. Sarah hesitated, frightened once again by the animal's eyes. Instead of going inside the stall, she raised the bucket gently over the partition.

"I'm ashamed of myself," she admitted softly.

"Well, that's all," the man said, setting down the bag of feed. "You better get yourself a chest or a closet or something to keep the feed in. A horse, if it can get itself into the oats, will eat itself to death."

As she paid him for the delivery of the horse and the things he had bought for her she felt that he had guessed it was she alone who would take care of the horse. And in his silence she felt his disapproval.

Sarah felt very discouraged as she went up to the attic to find something in which she could keep the feed. That morning she had burned what probably was the feed container. She was so afraid of her horse that it would be quite impossible for her to take care of it if it became sick. She didn't even know where she would get the courage to do all the necessary things such as feeding Gypsy. And as for riding her, only a miracle could help both of them.

An old plywood chest would have to do as a hiding place for the oats, she decided, and proceeded to carry the heavy thing down from the attic, across the house and into the stable.

Gypsy snorted.

"Your nose!" Sarah exclaimed letting the chest fall down. "It's not at all stuffed up!"

Before she realized what she had done, she was hugging the horse, holding its neck in both of her hands.

"Oh, Gypsy!" she cried and gently kissed the horse on its smooth neck. "I'm not afraid of you. I couldn't have hugged you if I were!"

It was true that she had not yet entered the stall; the planks of wood still separated them. But Sarah was very happy about her impulsive gesture. It was a beginning, she thought as she sat down on her rocking chair to rest.

"You must be patient with me," she said to her horse. "Give me a little time to get used to you. Why do you frighten me so? Is it your size? I don't know why I should be so afraid of getting near you. But I'll get over my fear. You must be patient. And I do promise you exercise! No matter how frightened, I shall ride you. And you are the most beautiful animal I've ever seen. I hope that one day you'll be as happy to have me as I am to have you."

The old woman's eyes closed for a minute, and when she opened them the horse was still looking at her.

"I'm so tired," Sarah said. "Would you mind if I took a little nap, right here? Maybe you'd like to go to sleep for a little while, too? We've had a big day already, and it's not even noon."

She watched the horse go back to its hay. She must have dozed off, because she did not hear the car drive up. What woke her was the sound of the horn and a voice shouting: "Hey, anyone home?"

She recognized Lee Earl's voice and got up fast. She would have hated anyone to see her asleep in the middle of the day and in a stable at that.

"Thank God!" she said in greeting. "I didn't even dare hope you'd come so soon. Oh, I do need you!"

"I gather the mare's here and you're frightened."

"Yes," she said, grateful that he had guessed. "The man who delivered her said that she might come down with shipping fever, and I don't seem to do anything right, and—"

"Let's take a look at her. By the way, did you find a name for her yet?"

"I called her Gypsy. Do you think it's appropriate?"

"Sounds like a fine name to me."

They walked together into the stable. She would ask this man about everything she could think of. She would ask him to show her how to saddle and how to ride the horse and how to take care of it.

"She's fine," Lee assured her after looking Gypsy over. "She won't get the fever."

"Thank God," Sarah whispered.

"It's a beautiful stable," Lee was saying, "and the stall is nice and large, but we must knock off this bench."

There was a long wooden bench along one of the sides, and she had planned to sit on it, once she got used to the horse.

"Why should we knock it off?" she wanted to know.

"Lots of horses like to lie down when they sleep. If

this one does, then she might get hurt on the bench. She'd be getting up, and she's liable to scratch herself badly, or even break a bone. Do you have a hammer?"

"Yes, in the house."

"Before we get it, let's look around. You'll be needing other things in here. Pliers to open the hay bales with if they are tied with wires, and large scissors or a knife for those tied with strings. You will also need a sponge to rub Gypsy down with, some soap, disinfectant, and deodorant to clean the stall with. By the way, do you have any water here?"

"No, but I've got a well just a few steps away. And then of course there is hot water in the house."

He leaned over the partition and looked into the stall.

"That bucket is too small. You need a wider one. How about the barn? There are probably some things in there that we can use."

They started walking toward it together. Sarah was surprised to see that David was sitting in the truck. She could barely see the outlines of his rather stubborn face, at once the face of a naughty child and a disappointed adult. He was leaning low over something she could not see.

"I didn't know David came with you."

"He did, but he didn't want to get out of the truck. He's got homework to do." Lee sighed. "I'm sorry for the way he behaved last night. I asked him about giving you horseback riding lessons, but he won't do it. He claims that he's got too much homework. But it's not that. He doesn't want to be around horses. You see, this year would have been the year we'd be working the rodeos together. Except, the last time I got hurt, David jumped in. That was the first time he'd ever done that."

He stopped for a moment, and his face turned away from her. Although his features were much sharper than his son's, the expression of his face was soft. She had not understood about David jumping into the arena, but she felt that Lee was telling her something very important.

"When he did that," Lee continued, "when he jumped in I shouldn't have even seen him. I had a job to do, and yet that's all I could see, and I almost got killed because I was looking at him and not at the bulls. In the hospital I realized that it would never work, our being together. Next time I'd watch him instead of the animals it might be one of the riders who'd get killed. I had to quit. It wouldn't be honest of me to let him come in with me. And he wasn't cut out for it either. He doesn't know fear, for one thing, never did, and that's bad. That would make him misjudge his chances. Well, when I quit I was doing it for both of us."

Again he stopped and Sarah waited for him to go

on. They were inside the barn now, and Lee began to look around it.

"Anyway," he added, "now he hates everything—the school, our house, his whole life—and he blames all his misery on me. And he can't even bear horses because they remind him of the life he isn't leading anymore."

"Do you think," she asked, "it would be all right for me to tell him that he is welcome to ride Gypsy any time he wants to?"

"That'd be mighty nice of you."

David, sitting in the truck, did not look at them when they passed him. He had brought his homework along, for he had to study for another test. It was important to him. If he flunked this one he'd have to go to summer school. Besides, he was sick and tired of other kids thinking he was stupid. But he couldn't concentrate. He was filled with self-pity, the kind that made his throat hurt and his eyes smart. And he was pitying himself because nothing at all was going right for him.

He had to study three times as hard as anyone else in school to keep up with the kids a year younger than he. While traveling with his father, he had learned how to read and write, and sometimes they would even buy some schoolbooks and he would study from them, but not really hard. Sometimes there would be a month or two when they would not have to go to rodeos. Then his father would send him to a school, never telling the principal that it would be for only a little while. During those times, David realized how much studying he had missed and how hard it would be to start going to school on a regular basis. But he never thought that he would have to do that. He'd be a clown soon. And knowing this was reason enough not to worry. He was frightened once when a truant officer talked to his father and told him about the law that a kid had to go to school. But no one could have caught up with them, traveling as they did. And no one asked questions after that one time.

But now, to keep up, he could never play baseball after school or hang around with other kids. Not that he really wanted to. It was only that he would have liked to have had a choice. But there was no choice. The other boys didn't even ask him, and he had to study—all the time, from the time he got home and made himself a sandwich, until past his bedtime, reading under the sheets by the beam of a flashlight, so his father would not know how hard it was for him.

And now the old woman and her horse! He had thought of them last night. He had promised himself that he would not hate the woman just because she had bought the horse he wanted. And he had promised himself that he would not think of the mare as *his* horse. But he thought that he might ride his bike over at night, when the moon was full, and give the mare a try. He'd like to do that often and in secret. Just because he didn't own the horse shouldn't prevent him from loving it. And besides, now his whole life was a secret one. He never talked to anyone. Least of all his father.

He bent down and read off the capitals of South America. Why did they have to study that? Did they have rodeos there? How thoughts like that made him mad! If he could only concentrate!

In the barn Lee and Sarah did find a box with some useful things, things which must have once belonged to her brother when he had a horse. There were a scraper, a hoof nail, and half a dozen folded feed bags, which Lee told her were the best things to rub a horse with to give it gloss. There were also a bottle of dried-up liniment, a jar of vaseline, and best of all, an old leather halter with a lead line. By the time they left the barn, Sarah had learned a lot about taking care of the horse, about grooming it and feeding it, and the general care of the stable. In one corner of the barn they found a bucket, just right for Gypsy. It hung on a bucket post, which also yielded a measuring cup for the oats. They took back a pitchfork, a shovel, pliers, and a wheelbarrow, which they filled with Gypsy's things.

Back in the stable Lee showed Sarah how to clean

after the horse, removing the minimum of straw with the manure, and airing and drying the wet straw in the sun so that it could be reused. Outside of the stable they discovered an overgrown compost hole. While she went to get the hammer Lee brought out of his truck a gift for her, two leather straps, which he attached to the side of the stable door.

"That's so you can saddle her comfortably. The straps snap on both sides of the halter, and she won't be shaking her head away when you fit the bit in her mouth."

"What would I do without you?" she said gratefully.

"You'd do all right. It would take you a little longer though." He opened the gate of the stall and took Gypsy out. "Now I'll show you how to saddle her."

She watched him, and when he was done he made her saddle the horse herself. She was afraid of tightening the girth, but he assured her it didn't hurt the horse.

"Most horses, especially mares, don't like the feel of it, and this one snapped her teeth, but it's not because it hurt. It will loosen up anyway, and most of the time you'll have to dismount after a while and tighten it again. It should be tight so the saddle don't move under you and rub off the hair on her back. The best way to see if it's tight enough and not too snug is to put two fingers between the girth and the belly."

She did as she was told, amazed at the horse's patience with them and at her own ease and lack of fear. She promised herself that she would have a treat for Gypsy each time she saddled her.

"Now for the bridle," Lee said.

When Sarah was trying to place the bit in the horse's mouth, Gypsy raised her head and turned it away from her.

"Always be firm with her," Lee said, prying Gypsy's mouth open with his fingers and slipping the bar in. "Be sure you put your fingers behind her teeth so that she can't bite you."

Lee took the horse out of the stable before mounting her. Without using the stirrups but with the help of the horn, he lifted himself up on the saddle. He held the reins quite loosely, and the horse did not throw him or run off with him as Sarah half expected.

"She is well behaved. That I'll say for her," Lee said. "And she looked almost too good when David rode her in the auction barn. But you watch us now. I'll first make her walk, then jog and lope, and I'll see how she does on turns."

Without knowing anything at all about riding, Sarah realized that Lee was a fine horseman. Gypsy's eagerness to take off was equally evident, but she was being kept in check, and only her slightly tossing head and her high-stepping feet indicated that she would have been much happier if she did not have to walk. Her jog was smooth, Lee sitting firmly in the saddle, and when they did take off at a lope and then a gallop, Sarah caught her breath, it seemed so fast. It was marvelous to watch them, the grace of the horse and the ability of the man.

"She is fast!" Lee exclaimed, bringing her to a halt in front of Sarah. "She is in fine shape, much better than I thought she'd be in. Now we shall see how she does on the turns."

He took her on the grass and, loping, made a very sharp turn to the left by using the reins on her neck only slightly. Gypsy turned, changing leads beautifully, her whole body coming around after her inside legs had made the turns.

David had been watching from the truck. Grudgingly he had to admit to himself that his father was a darn good rider. He still looked as if he were a champion bronco rider and roper. He could always do anything with a horse, whether a tame or a wild one. He remembered one day, out in Arizona, when his father was breaking in a black stallion that one of the men had caught in a canyon after a two-day chase. The stallion had already thrown and hurt a half dozen men before his father got on him. It took him less than an hour to make a lamb out of that ornery critter. He had let David ride him afterward, and the owner, having come back from the hospital

with a cast on one of his arms, couldn't get over it—
how Lee could have done the impossible in such a
short time.

Now with Gypsy he was making her look as good
as David thought she would be. He lowered his eyes
back to the book when he heard his father shout to
the old woman, "By golly, the old mare must have
been a barrel horse once!" That's what David had
suspected from the speed of her turns in the auction
barn.

"What's a barrel horse?" the woman shouted back,
and David couldn't help smiling at the note of plea-
sure in her voice.

"A rodeo horse that makes turns around a barrel,"
Lee shouted as he brought Gypsy around in a neat
figure eight. Then he backed her up, using a loose
rein and just talking to her. "You ought to keep her
trained so she don't forget what she's learned so
well."

It is a miraculous thing, Sarah thought to herself,
for me to buy a horse like that, a horse so perfect. Lee
walked Gypsy over to where she was standing. The
horse's chest and shoulders were darker now; she had
sweated, and her light chestnut had become quite
brown, so the cut-off mane looked twice as light
against the darkened hide.

"Now it's your turn," Lee said, and Sarah's throat
tightened with fear.

"Hey," Lee exclaimed, "you're wearing a dress,

for goodness' sake! Go on and change into a pair of slacks."

"But she seems so exhausted," Sarah protested. "Look, she's sweating so."

"That's good!" Lee said. "They all sweat after a little exercise. And mind you, this is just a little exercise that I've given her. In her condition you can ride her two, three hours and she'll be fine."

It was no use. She went toward the house to change. On the way she stopped by the truck.

"Hello, David," she said warmly to the boy who was pretending to read his book.

"Hello," he said and looked at her. "That's a mighty nice horse you have."

"Oh, David, I'm so happy you think so too." She was glad to see that he didn't look quite so dismal. His face was still set in hard lines, but his eyes were not as somber. "I called her Gypsy but what I actually wanted to do was ask you about naming her. I wanted to do that last night at the auction, but you went away without even giving me a chance to thank you for the demonstration."

"Gypsy's all right for her name," David said. "I'm bad at naming things, anyway."

"I want you to know that you can come and ride Gypsy any time you wish. Each day, if you want."

"It's your horse," he said. "You shouldn't want anyone to ride her."

"But I do. I do want you to ride her!"

"I wouldn't," he said and looked down at the book, and then again at her. There was a sudden, unexpected warmth between them; his face relaxed completely and he looked like a little boy rather than a young man. "I mean, I'd rather not fool around with someone else's horse. One day I might have a horse of my own."

He didn't know why he had said this. He hadn't meant to say anything at all and he felt strangely confused, especially because the woman had smiled at him and then, without another word, walked away.

Somewhere in her closet there was a pair of old slacks she hardly ever wore. Her husband hadn't liked to see a woman wearing pants and used to say, "Practically every female born has a good pair of legs and only the foolish ones would want to hide what nature took a long time to perfect."

While she was changing, Lee walked Gypsy over to the truck. David pretended he didn't see his father come up.

"You won't change your mind?"

"About what?" He knew very well what his father was talking about.

"About giving Mrs. Tierney some lessons. She sure could use some. It will be very easy for her to ruin this good horse if she don't know what to do. I know she'll spoil her in the worst way, and if she don't know how to ride, then Gypsy will take over completely and within two months she won't be the same horse."

"I'm sorry," David said.

"How about a reason?" his father asked. "Don't you even want to give me one?"

"I've got homework to do," David said impatiently, his eyes on the book. "You don't realize how much I have."

"And that's it?"

"Sure, that's it."

His father stood by the side of the truck for a while and then walked slowly away, Gypsy following him.

Sarah's heart was beating furiously and her throat was parched with fear. Lee was shortening the stirrups for her, and she wished she could tell him how afraid she was.

"You've got yourself a fine western horse here," Lee said. "Get yourself some western gear—blue jeans and cowboy boots. You can skip the ten-gallon hat."

"I'll do that," she managed to say.

"I won't be around to give you a leg up, so let's see if you can make it up all by yourself."

He told her how to approach the horse always from the left side and how to swing herself up with the help of the saddle horn. She was surprised that she managed to get on quite easily. He had held on to the reins while she was mounting, but once she was seated, he gave her the reins and Gypsy started to walk away down the road.

"You seem to have a good pair of hands," Lee said as he walked beside her.

The fear had not left her, but she knew this was the time to try her horse out, with Lee around. She loosened the reins a little, and the second she did, Gypsy took off at a fast canter. Sarah was petrified by the speed and her distance from the ground, and she held on to the horn with one hand. Off they went, faster now, at a gallop, down the dirt road.

I'll never be able to make her stop, Sarah thought. We'll be galloping down the highway for the rest of our lives. But it was Gypsy who slowed down before reaching the road. She turned around, fast, and Sarah managed to keep her seat. On the way back, at a canter, she even let go of the horn and began to enjoy the ride. Gypsy stopped in front of Lee and stood shaking her head proudly.

"I don't think," Lee said, "that I should worry about you two females. You did fine."

"But I was terrified," Sarah said laughing.

"Everyone is, at first."

Sarah leaned over and patted Gypsy's neck.

"And I didn't do anything at all. It was she who took me for a ride."

"Well, don't let her get into that habit. You must let her know who is master."

"I'm afraid she already does know. She is."

"No!" Lee said firmly. "You are. And talk to her. That's the best way I know of to get a horse used to you. And you should use your reins, across her neck for directions, and slack when you want her to run, and tighter when you want her to walk."

"How do I stop her?"

"Pull up on the reins, then slacken them, then pull again, and if you must, say Whoa."

Sarah got off by herself and stood proudly looking at her mount.

"She is beautiful, isn't she?"

"Yes," Lee said, "she is a wonderful horse. But now we must walk her to cool her off."

He told her how she should check by feeling under the horse's chest whether the horse had cooled off, and he told her other things: about putting a blanket on Gypsy on a windy day, about picking her feet for stones, how long and how often to groom her, why she should never be fed after being ridden, and how much water it is safe to give a horse when it is still warm.

When they left, Sarah was alone with Gypsy. She stood for a long time leaning against the fence, looking at her horse grazing on the new grass. And in the newness of the spring, the newness of her possession, she felt the renewal of her own life. Her world was once again complete. She belonged to someone and someone belonged to her.

Chapter Five

Waking up, Sarah Tierney was aware of having dreamt about her horse. Lying in bed trying to recall what it was that she had dreamt about was no use. She never was able to remember dreams, and she had always envied people who could. Dressing hurriedly, she wondered how Gypsy had spent the night. She had said a long good-bye to her horse, unwilling to leave her alone for the night. And now she was eager to see her again.

She noticed right away that Gypsy had been lying down during the night; straw was clinging to one side of her coat. With a shiver of apprehension Sarah went inside the stall to brush her, but realized that she should feed her first.

"I'm sorry," she whispered. "I will brush you as you eat. That way I don't think you'll object to my being so close to you."

She got the grain and spilled it into the feeder. Gypsy ate hungrily while Sarah spoke to her gently as she brushed her coat with the curry comb and then with the large brush. When she was through, she waited for her horse to finish eating. She could not resist the gloss of the coat, and leaned against it, burying her face in the softness of it.

"I'll put you out in the pasture," she said to Gypsy as she was leading her out of the stall. "It's a beautiful morning and the sun is warm. Later, in a few days, I'll let you roam around free. You can feed then on the lawn, in front of the house, on the grass under the maple trees, and anywhere else you'll choose to go. But you must realize that this is your home now and that you cannot run away from me."

When Gypsy was being led out of the stable, Sarah's fingers slipped from the halter and the horse walked off. When Sarah ran after her, Gypsy took off, cantering down the road with her mistress running behind her calling her name.

I'll never catch her, Sarah thought desperately. She'll be killed on the highway.

But still she ran, breathless now, and crying, when Gypsy disappeared around the curve. The driveway was long, and by the time Sarah reached the highway her heart was pounding wildly. She had been listening for the sound of trucks or cars, petrified that Gypsy would run into the heavy traffic. But there were no cars. She looked up and down the long stretch of the highway, almost flat for a quarter of a mile in each direction, but she did not see her horse. She turned around to run back to the house and get her car, when she saw the copper of Gypsy's body, half hidden by a bush. She could have shouted for joy but controlled herself and approached the horse cautiously. Gypsy raised her head and looked at the woman with her blue eye, and did not run away but continued to graze on the grassy spot between the dirt road and the highway. Sarah got hold of the halter, very firmly this time.

Before leading her back, she rubbed her forehead on Gypsy's neck, and half laughing, scolded her. "Don't you know you've frightened me half to death? Or did you just want to give me some exercise? I'm an old woman, not a girl, and you must remember that. You must never do that again."

Gypsy nodded her head and snorted. Sarah led her back up the road, stopping occasionally to kiss her on the neck.

They walked together, the horse alert to everything around her, moving her head from side to side, sometimes looking at the woman with a sidelong glance, her ears quivering to the sound of her mistress' voice and the other sounds around them, the birds and the branches moving in the breeze.

With Gypsy safely in the pasture, Sarah stood leaning against the fence. She could stand for hours talking to Gypsy and watching her, but she knew she shouldn't do that. She had a house to take care of and the stable to clean. First things first, she said to herself, going into the stable. She decided to buy some carrots and apples in town before she gave Gypsy her exercise, and reward her with them if she was good.

While trying to do her chores inside the house, she kept going to the south windows, from where she could see Gypsy in the pasture. At one point she saw her lie down, as if collapsing, and her heart came to a standstill at the thought that she had gotten sick, but Gypsy immediately rolled on the grass a few times, then stood up and shook herself like a dog when it's wet. Sarah laughed and then, unable to resist the temptation, she ran out of the house and into the pasture to put her arms around the feeding horse's neck.

Although reluctant to leave Gypsy, Sarah drove into town to buy a pair of blue jeans and order her cowboy boots, and pick up the apples and carrots for her horse. When she was parking her car, John Connors, the garbage man, put his head in the window.

"Hi, there, Mrs. Tierney," he greeted her. "Hear you got yourself a horse."

She was surprised. "Who told you?"

"Forgot who it was, but it's true, ain't it?"

"Yes," she admitted.

"My brother had a horse once," John Connors said. "It was crazy about lettuce."

"Oh," Sarah said, "I'll have to buy mine some."

"Too expensive," John Connors said. "I'll tell you what I'll do for you. Twice a week on my rounds, I'll stop by your house and leave you lettuce trimmings. They throw them out in stores and supermarkets. I'll just ask the boys to put the lettuce in separate boxes. How's that?"

"Oh, that's very kind of you, John," Sarah said gratefully.

At the dry-goods store Tom Straka, the owner, said to her when she was hardly inside the door:

"Ordered you some cowboy boots. They ought to be here about the middle of next week."

"How did you know?"

"Word gets around."

"I suppose"—she smiled at him—"that you also knew I needed some blue jeans."

"There's a couple of pairs for you to try on in the back room."

In the grocery store where she went for the apples and carrots, Jean, the young clerk, had a big box of apples waiting for her.

"These here apples aren't rotten or anything," she

said, "but they're sort of spotted, so you can have the whole box for ten cents."

Sarah laughed.

"You didn't know I also wanted some carrots, did you?"

"Sure," she said, "there's a bag of them here. I asked Sam to give you a special wholesale rate on them."

On the street she thought that everyone smiled at her more kindly than usually, and she was happy that no one laughed at her or questioned her about her horse.

It was after two in the afternoon when she finally got Gypsy saddled. She had no trouble putting the bridle on, but she had to retie the saddle knot twice before she got it right. She was nervous and scared as she got Gypsy out of the stable and mounted her.

"Now," she said, "you've had one carrot and one apple. You'll have two of each if you walk nicely." She kept repeating the order to walk, and her horse obeyed. But she didn't know whether the obedience was due to her command or to the path they took. It was narrow and followed a winding creek. The patches of moist grass and the stones made for careful stepping. "This is what we'll always do first," Sarah said, patting the horse's neck. "We'll walk right here. It's beautiful and you wouldn't want to run here. But I do hope that your feet don't hurt because of the stones. I must ask Lee about that."

It was truly a beautiful walk. The path was shady, with the sun visible only in rays of light, cool with the moisture of the water and green with the new foliage. They were walking up to the top of a hill, and Sarah had to dodge the branches by putting her face next to the horse's neck. The feeling of fear did not vanish, but during the walk it subsided. And talking to the horse, she realized, was the fastest way of pushing the fear away.

The hill had a flat plateau, and it was here that Sarah tried to make Gypsy do her turns. She remembered how Lee leaned slightly toward the side he was turning to and how he placed the reins on the horse's neck.

"Now, barrel horse, do your stuff," Sarah whispered in Gypsy's ear. Amazingly enough the horse obeyed the neck reining quite well. At first, however, it did the turns at barely a trot and Sarah bounced up and down in the saddle, not liking it a bit. She loosened the reins and said, "All right," and Gypsy broke into a canter. After a pat on the neck and high praise, Sarah let the horse do what it wanted. And it wanted to run. They cantered out of the shade cast by the maple trees and into the sunlit fields and down a grassy road. Gypsy broke into a gallop, and Sarah loved the speed and the feeling of freedom that came with it. Her eyes filled with tears from the wind.

They reached another hill and they stood motionless for a while, the horse and the woman both look-ing down into the valley below them. They could see the house and the barn but not the stable, and beyond the winding dirt road, the highway. And on the four sides of them there lay the land that Sarah owned, fields coming alive with the new green of grass, and to the north, the green roof of the maple grove.

"It is a beautiful place, isn't it?" Sarah said to Gypsy. "Look out there. Do you see that smoke? Be-sides the smoke, all you can see of Cornwall is the spire of the church. We'll ride there one day. I'll have to show you off sometime to all those people who know about you. Once I stop being afraid, we'll have so much fun together!"

By the time they returned to the stable, Sarah felt that she had gotten to know her land much better than ever before. And it was Gypsy who taught her how to look at it. Gypsy was constantly aware of everything around her. For the first time in her life Sarah noticed the beauty of the light playing on the ground. She heard the music of the cracking branches and the moving leaves, the timid noise of a bird un-willing to fly off, and the powerful swish of the wings from those that took flight at the sound of the hoofs. She looked at the rabbits standing and then taking off, and she even saw a deer staring back at them, motionless; and she was glad that Gypsy feared nothing but noticed everything.

Ever since her marriage the coming of spring had filled her with an acute realization of happiness. The feeling of belonging intensified for her in the springtime. It was as if the renewal of nature welded her closer to the land and to everything she held dear. This, her first spring without Paul, was not going to be different. This spring it was Gypsy who was making the wonder of spring once again miraculous for Sarah.

Chapter Six

It was no use. The harder David stared at the questions, the harder they seemed. Looking out of the window was no help either, and noticing that Miss MacKean, his teacher, was glancing at him worriedly made it all much worse. He wasn't even sure if any of the test questions, except one, were answered in his book. I must be stupid, he decided angrily.

There were only five kids besides him in the seventh grade, and most of them looked so much younger than he that that alone could spoil his day. Even if he didn't dislike them all he couldn't imagine any of them becoming his friends. The twins, who had already handed in their test papers, were the only ones who tried to find out anything about him; the others weren't even interested in where he came from. The two boys, whom no one could tell apart, were now looking toward him, and they, like Miss MacKean, looked worried. He bent down over the paper, and this time he just tried to guess at the answers.

If only they wanted to know something about the rodeo! If only, instead of South America, they could be studying about George Washington. Of course not the George Washington who was the first President of the United States, but the Negro of that name who in Canadian, Texas, one day in 1880 got on a bucking bronco and rode him right out of the arena and down the railroad tracks all the way to the depot. Or he could tell them about Thad Sowder, a real hero, a kind of hero they should be studying about in school anyway. He was about the greatest rodeo figure around the turn of the century. In later years when Thad was paralyzed and penniless—for in those days bravery was paid more with fame than with money—he ended his days peddling pillow covers carrying his picture as the world's champion broncobuster. David even had been to Thad's grave in Ovid, Colorado. He had made his father take him there one winter. And if they wanted names, why couldn't they be asking who Tom Threepersons was? He was a Cherokee, and there was no greater Indian in rodeo than Tom.

And how about Yakima Canutt, John Rock, Earl Thode, Pete Knight, Doff Aber? Of course they were all dead now and lay buried in lonely grave-yards out West, but that was no reason to forget them. They were, after all, a heck of a lot more important than whatever it was that was exported from Ecuador.

And whoever Magellan might have been, he couldn't have been half the man Jazzbo Fulkerson was. Jazzbo was the first rodeo clown to use the barrel. He devised it to give the bull a hard target to hit. He fashioned it out of a steel drum with rubber tires around it, and he would crawl into it and all curled up would wait for the terrifying crash of the animal's impact. If they would only ask David how many bruises and how many gorings Jazzbo had suffered he'd be able to tell them. And he could tell them about the time a bull's horn took one of Jazzbo's eyes and how Jazzbo came back into the arena in three months to work again, a one-eyed, fear-less clown who delighted the ones who didn't know about the danger and petrified the ones who did. And he could tell them about Jimmy Schumacher, and about the time he got twenty-four stitches after one horn wound, plus broken collarbones, legs, and ribs, and a mangled foot.

As the bell rang for recess David was sure that he was not stupid. He knew a lot more names and a lot more dates than all the other kids put together. It was just that they were names and dates no one in school seemed to care about.

And knowing that he wasn't really stupid was responsible for the fight that he got into that morning.

"The dummy didn't know any answers," he heard Peter Pollock say behind his back. David didn't want to ask for an apology, but swung out with both fists at the boy. It didn't even matter that Peter was smaller and that David had once promised himself never to hit a smaller kid. They rolled in the mud of the schoolyard, hitting each other, until the cries of the other children brought Miss MacKean.

David followed his teacher to the classroom. She did not speak until she reached her desk and sat down. Then she looked at him, and her blue eyes were dark with anger.

"David," she said, "I cannot allow such behavior from you. I had great hopes for you. When you came in that first day, I thought that you would be one of the few students I'd remember when I grew old. You have been a complete disappointment to me."

She lifted his test paper from her desk and held it at arm's length.

"This was to be more than a test," she continued while David looked down at his muddied shoes. "This was going to prove to me whether or not you'd pass to the eighth grade without going to summer school. Well,"—she slammed her hand down and let go of his test—"you had one, a single, answer right." She waited for him to say something and when he did not, she cleared her throat and more calmly asked, "What is your explanation? First for the fight, and then for your failure to answer the questions correctly."

It would have been much better had she just hit him, or punished him, but she had to choose the hardest thing, questioning. One thing he could not do was to tell her he hit Peter for calling him a dummy.

"Well?"

"I don't know," he said very quietly. "I don't know why I got into the fight."

"Did Peter say something to you?"

He didn't answer.

"I shall find out about that from the other children. Now, tell me, did you or did you not study for the test?"

"I did."

"But if you did, how come you did not know the answers?"

"It must be," he said, "that I can't concentrate."

She sat down at her desk, and he looked up at her, hoping that the answer had satisfied her. He was sorry for her for caring for him and the others, for being a teacher.

"Would you want to tell me anything?" she asked softly. "Maybe you have a problem I could help you with. Maybe all you need is talking to someone. I know how it is sometimes. I was brought up without a mother, too."

He wished she'd leave him alone, and yet he could not be angry at her for wanting to help him.

"I'll be all right," he said. "I'll just have to try harder, that's all."

"Well, David,"—the bell rang when she said this—"I'm here to help you. Anytime you feel like talking. And I do believe you about wanting to try harder."

David was grateful to her. But he felt more discouraged than ever, for he really had been trying.

Chapter Seven

⊂ ∩ "Well!" No one who had ever heard Margaret Evans' voice could ever forget it, it was that unpleasant. "Sarah! I've been calling you all day yesterday and today!" She waited for an explanation, but receiving none, continued: "Of course *I* don't believe it! I *refuse* to believe silly gossip about you going off and getting yourself a horse! Are you there, Sarah?"

"Yes, Margaret," Sarah said with a sigh, "I'm here."

"Well! You were not at choir practice!"

"Oh, I forgot all about it," Sarah said and then, making a sudden decision, she added, "I won't be coming to sing in the choir anymore."

"What!"

"I shall call Father Connen and tell him I can't be in the choir since I no longer have the time for practice."

There was an ominous silence on the other end of the wire, and Sarah smiled to herself because she could, in her mind's eye, see the expression of outraged fury on Margaret's face. She had known Margaret Evans for more years than she cared to recall. They had gone through school together, and even before that they used to play together. Margaret had not changed in all those years; even as a child she was much too bossy, too quick to anger over unimportant things. For the last forty years Margaret's main preoccupation had been the church choir. She played the organ and was in charge of the choir composed of the ladies of the parish. Periodically Margaret Evans tried to enlist young people and men into the choir, but the young people didn't seem to like her, and the men were openly terrified of her. The choir, never too pleasantly in harmony, had become dreadful in the last few years.

"Sarah Tierney!" Margaret exploded into the telephone. "I never would have thought *you* capable of such treachery!"

"But Margaret—"

"Don't Margaret me! Then it's true. You did get a horse, didn't you?"

"Yes, Margaret, I did get a horse and it will keep me much too busy."

"And *I* refused to believe it!" Margaret screeched. "What in heaven's name possessed you to do such a stupid thing?"

Sarah looked out of the window. She could see her horse lying down in the grass, its eyes shut to the rays of the sun. She smiled at the beautiful sight of that big copper body on the green of the pasture.

"Sarah! Why don't you answer me!"

"What do you want me to say, Margaret?"

"Well! Give me an explanation if you *can!*"

"There is no use talking," Sarah said quietly. Her patience was beginning to wear thin. "You're much too excited and angry—"

"Wouldn't you be excited and angry," Margaret shouted, "if you found out your best friend was making an utter fool of herself? A horse! At your age!"

Sarah Tierney had never suspected that Margaret considered her her best friend. She was touched by this unexpected confession. It was in a much milder tone that she spoke.

"Margaret, you have no idea what a joy this horse is to me."

"A joy?"

"Yes, a perfect joy. I wish you'd get a horse too."

"Stop it, Sarah!"

"You really should get a horse," Sarah repeated with a smile. "It's so wonderful!"

"Please spare me your mad suggestions. And Sarah, I'll never, never forgive you if that *beast* comes between us! We need you in the choir, and you *cannot* desert us now, not before Easter."

"I'm sorry, Margaret, but I will have to. I'm sure you'll get along without me."

Margaret could not have heard all of Sarah's last sentence. The hum on the other line told Sarah that her friend had hung up.

Sarah thought of saddling Gypsy and going for a ride, but instead she sat at the window and watched her horse graze. She thought about the changes that had come over Cornwall in the past years. When she was a girl the town was full of eager young people. But since World War II the population had begun to decline. The younger people were the first to leave, but now even the middle-aged ones were going away. The ones who stayed were either old or did not have children. Cornwall, except for Main Street, gave the impression of a ghost town. Beautiful old houses, with turrets and fancy woodcarving decorating the windows, stood abandoned. Some with their windows broken, like wounds, others with shutters that swayed in the wind and doors half ajar, looked like people living in the past and unconscious of the present. Where once lawns were kept immaculately free of weeds, now brush grew, forbidding entrance to houses inhabited only by ever dimmer ghosts of sounds and sights.

In a way Margaret was like Cornwall. She had not

changed much over the years; yet her years of aloneness had carved a bitterness into her. The desolation
of her loveless life was as sad as the desolation of the
houses. And she, like Cornwall, was once very young,
and almost pretty. But now, like the town, she ap-
peared as forbidding as a past without a future.

Sarah's thoughts were interrupted by the arrival of
Father Francis Connen. She heard his old Ford a long
way off. It had lost its exhaust pipe a long time ago,
and its asthmatic motor was well known to everyone.
She wondered if he had come to talk her into staying
on with the choir. She liked the young priest very
much, and it would be terribly difficult for her to
refuse him anything. "She's a beauty!" Father Connen was saying over his shoulder as he patted Gypsy,
who came to the fence to greet him. "How does she
behave when you ride her?"

"Pretty well so far, Father," Sarah answered, "but
I'm afraid that the longer I have her, the more spoiled
she'll become."

"Do you ride her western?"

"Yes, Father."

"Would you mind if I tried her out?"

"Of course not!" She was surprised that he rode.
But she was even more surprised when he only put
the bridle on Gypsy and jumped on her bareback.

"I've never ridden with a saddle on," he explained.
"And don't worry, Mrs. Tierney. We'll take it easy. I

know all about walking the horse for the first mile. But I don't promise you that I won't give her a fair amount of exercise."

Sarah stood looking after them—the priest in his shiny black suit sitting straight and proud, Gypsy prancing high. It must be wonderful, she thought, to ride a horse bareback, but I'm afraid I'll never be able to do that. I will keep on holding to the horn of that saddle for safety. I'll never get over this fear.

The priest came back toward her, holding Gypsy easily, the reins loose, the horse walking now without nervousness.

"If you go to my car," Father Connen said, "you'll find a copy of *The Horseman's Encyclopedia* on the front seat. I brought it for you. I think it's tired of being wedged between *The Life of St. Anne* and *Reflections on Spiritual Life*. I hope you'll find it as profitable as I did when I had a horse."

Before she had a chance to thank him, he let Gypsy trot away. Even at a trot, she marveled, he kept his seat. She got the book out and looked through it, and was very happy to discover that it contained a tremendous amount of information about horses, their care, and how to ride them. She began to read it, starting with "Accidents," and was on "Harness Racing" when Father Connen returned. Gypsy was in a lather and Father Connen was exclaiming, "What a wonderful horse! What a truly wonderful horse!"

Together they walked to cool Gypsy off.

"Margaret Evans called me," Father Connen said, "and of course she went on and on about your quitting the choir."

"I've always hated it," Sarah said with a smile, "and now that I've got such a perfect excuse—"

"I don't blame you. I too hate that miserable choir." They both laughed. "Don't give it another thought. I only hope that with you gone maybe they'll start dissolving the whole thing. I've never had enough courage to ask them to. I'll try to talk to Margaret and suggest she just play the organ and forget about those voices."

"I'll help you talk her into it as soon as she has a chance to forget how mad she is at me."

"I wish you would. With both of us making the same request, maybe she'll give in." He patted Gypsy's neck. "I'm terribly happy for you. You got yourself a wonderful animal."

"If you wish, Father, come and ride her. Any time at all. Every day if you can."

"Thank you but I'm afraid I won't be able to right now. There is the north wall of the church which has to be rebuilt if we intend to have it there for next winter. You know, I had a horse once, when I was only ten. At that age I hoped I wouldn't grow another inch. I wanted very badly to be a jockey. But at eleven I shot up a couple of inches, and by the time I was fourteen I was already almost six feet tall. And instead of being a small jockey, God willed me to be a tall priest. But Gypsy is fast! She is incredibly fast. I do believe she's been raced! She's got a lot of quarter horse in her, and if she came from out West, I imagine she raced with the quarter horses."

"How do the quarter horses race?" Sarah wanted to know. She really meant to ask what the difference was between a quarter horse and a thoroughbred, but she thought she would look it up in her encyclopedia.

"They race for only a quarter of a mile. That's where their name comes from. They're good and fast, but don't have the stamina or the long legs the thoroughbreds have, and that's why they can't take longer stretches."

Later that afternoon Sarah sat in her rocking chair reading the *Encyclopedia* while Gypsy ate her lettuce trimmings. Although Sarah had not ridden her horse that day, the third day, she felt tired and closed her eyes. As it was now her habit to do, she fell asleep and awoke past Gypsy's and her dinnertime.

The moon was not full but it was light enough. Especially for Gypsy's watch eye it was light enough. David pedaled hard the eight miles that separated him from Gypsy's stable. The house was dark. The woman would be asleep. It was well after midnight. Gypsy greeted him with a low sound of anticipation. He found the oats and gave her a handful.

"If I hadn't been so stubborn," he whispered to her

as she licked his hand clean, "you'd be my horse and not hers."

He led Gypsy out of the box stall after putting on the bridle. He would not use the saddle. Saddles were for a working cowboy; they were useful for roping and for when one had to ride for hours. He led Gypsy, holding her, not riding her, on the grass beside the driveway. Halfway, when they were far enough away for the woman not to hear the hoofbeats, he jumped on her and held her to a walk until they reached the road. It would be safer to ride her there, along the grassy patch, where he knew there were no holes and no stones. It was a long time since he had ridden. Now the wind was chasing them and they were chasing the wind into the night. And it seemed more like flying—like being a bird—than ever before, with Gypsy beneath him, her strides even, her eagerness to run as great as his own.

He didn't know when he began to cry or why. Maybe because he loved that horse and knew his father had really tried to make things up to him. But tears were blinding him. He wetted Gypsy's neck with them as he walked her after their ride, his face buried in her short mane.

"It can't be you now," he whispered to her, "but I'll have me a horse like you one day."

He made sure that she was dry and cool before putting her back into the stall. He gave her some more hay and cleaned her bed for her and kissed her good night. On the way back he sang. For the first time since they'd moved to Vermont he was happy enough to sing.

Chapter Eight

The nearness of the horse ceased to frighten Sarah within a week, but more than three weeks passed before she got over her fear of riding. The day she saddled and rode Gypsy without the familiar tightening sensation in the pit of her stomach was the day she went to Burlington and bought a hackamore.

She had read in the *Horseman's Encyclopedia* that a hackamore was easiest on a horse that resented a metal bar in its mouth. A leather strap over the horse's nose would tighten slightly at the pressure of a pulled rein, and the horse would follow the commands. Now when she saddled Gypsy, the horse accepted the bridle without tossing her head. And with her mouth free, Gypsy seemed to enjoy their daily rides as much as her mistress.

With the fear gone there opened a new world of enjoyment for Sarah. The love she felt for Gypsy was an ever growing thing. It seemed to her that now she inhabited a sort of a kingdom, a wondrous country fashioned by mutual need, hers and Gypsy's. It was a kingdom yet to be explored. She had only reached the first of its many turreted castles, and each day, with each new experience, both of them seemed to venture further. And it was Gypsy who was always leading the way on that splendid journey.

They had a routine now. After a short walk Sarah would make Gypsy do her turns on the flat top of a nearby hill. Some days the horse flatly refused to change leads, pretending she didn't know what was wanted of her.

"You're not fooling anyone," Sarah would say. "You're just plain lazy."

Gypsy's tossing neck would seem to agree with her, and Sarah would not insist. She would wait for those days which seemed right to Gypsy to practice what she had once been taught.

What Gypsy and Sarah both liked best of all was to run. They would gallop for a quarter of a mile, Gypsy snorting happily, the wind filling Sarah's eyes with tears. They rode as though they were racing against an invisible string of horses. The earth moved away from them, the grass lay trampled in their wake, the birds competed with them in this flight through the sunlit fields and up the shade of the grassy road. On the top of the hill Gypsy would come to a stop, without a command. There Sarah would dismount and let the horse graze while she looked at the incredible beauty of the countryside. It never ceased to amaze her. It was ever changing, ever more dazzling.

Many times they chased a rabbit across the fields, and once a buck deer. And now, with the fear gone, Sarah would take her horse to Cornwall once a week. A patch of grass on both sides lined the road, and Gypsy would gallop or canter most of the two miles, not at all afraid of the passing cars. When they would arrive at the town sign, with its ever diminishing population recorded faithfully every year, Gypsy would slow down to a walk. While Sarah would go to the post office or the bank, Gypsy would stand, tied to a parking meter, looking at the goings on and letting passers-by pet her. Sarah had not been ashamed, even that first time, to ride down Main Street. She didn't care if anyone laughed at her, and no one did laugh. She knew that some people, those who had listened to Margaret Evans, continued to think her quite mad, but the fact was that her decision to buy a horse was the very best she had made in many years.

"Well." It was Margaret Evans, looking down her nose. She was standing at her box in the post office, and Sarah Tierney saw that there was nothing inside of the box.

"Hello, Margaret," she said warmly. "How is the choir?"

"Why would *you* care?" Margaret shot back, slamming the little door of her box shut.

"But I do care! About *you* anyway."

"We're not going to have a choir. I'll just be playing the organ at the ten o'clock mass."

"I think that's wonderful! You play so well, and the voices used to drown your lovely music. Oh, I'm so happy!"

Margaret coughed.

"I'll finally be able to play Bach," she said.

Sarah smiled. "Wonderful!" She put her arm around Margaret. "Come out and meet Gypsy."

"Does one get introduced to horses nowadays?" Margaret asked.

"It's the latest thing," Sarah said.

Whatever reluctance there might have been on Margaret's part vanished at the sight of the horse, and when Gypsy nuzzled Margaret, she invited her home for lunch.

"You can come, too," Margaret said to Sarah, "but you'll have to settle for less than apples, pears and carrots."

After that Margaret would often come and watch her friend cleaning the stable, massaging Gypsy's legs with a mixture of water, vinegar, and liniment, soaking her feet in a bucket of water with Epsom salts, and grooming her. Gypsy's coat now shone with a russet glow, her mane and tail were growing, and she had put on the needed pounds.

"I don't know about this particular toothpaste," Sarah said one day while brushing Gypsy's teeth. "I tried it myself and didn't care for the taste of it."

Margaret laughed. "If there is still a place," she said, "where they worship horses, you might find the competition rather keen, but in the Christian world I am sure there is no other horse more pampered than this old mare of yours."

One day, after seeing her friend ride, Margaret asked, "Would you mind letting me try?"

Sarah looked at her with amazement. "You? On a horse?"

"My skirt is wide enough for an elephant, so what seems to be the problem?"

She mounted by herself and did quite well at a walk, even better at a canter, always in full control of the animal, and seated more firmly in the saddle than Sarah.

"Where in heaven's name did you learn to ride? I've known you all my life."

"Except for one summer," Margaret Evans reminded her. "The summer I went to Colorado to visit my aunt."

"That was when you were fourteen, wasn't it?"

"Fifteen."

"And you rode out there?"

"Not only did I ride. I was given a horse."

"You never told me!"

"No, I never did."

"But what happened? Why didn't you bring the horse back to Cornwall with you?"

Margaret Evans passed her hand gently over Gypsy's neck. "I never brought it back,"—her voice was not the harsh one everyone knew; it was now low and sweet sounding—"because the day we were going to leave, my horse broke a leg." She paused and then added very quickly, "I had to shoot it."

"And you shot it yourself?"

"Yes, I shot it! It was my horse and it was I who had to do it. And that's why I would never have another. And also that is why I was so mean when I found you'd bought a horse."

Summer came and with it the fight against flies. The stable had to be sprayed and Gypsy rubbed down with a fly repellent. They would go out now in the early morning or very late in the afternoon, not because of the Vermont heat but because of the deer-flies that seemed never to tire in their attack.

But summer was also a time of fun. For Gypsy it was the time of roaming free. She was no longer locked in the pasture behind a fence, but was given the freedom to go where she pleased. It was a time of rolling in the fragrant grass, of lying down for a sunbath and a morning nap amidst the clover. It was a time of long days and short nights, a time of warmth and security.

For Sarah it was a time of discovery. She discovered that Gypsy did not mind at all sharing her hours of sunbathing. She would lie down alongside her horse, using its neck for a pillow, and fall asleep under the warm sun. She discovered Gypsy's willingness to come into the house, and the kitchen became the place where both of them would have their afternoon snacks, Gypsy a bowlful of quartered apples and carrots and Sarah her tea. Often that summer Sarah would spend nights in the stable, sleeping on a cot, loving to see her horse lie down for the night, the great copper body in repose, deerlike in its beauty. Before falling asleep they would listen to the radio. Gypsy's ears were only alert when jazz or popular songs were being played, but she seemed to pay no attention whatever to the news or the weather.

That summer, during their time of quiet happiness, Sarah also discovered that being a creature of habit she was very much like her horse. And both of them seemed to relish the tranquility of their existence.

For David it was the worst of summers. There was summer school and all that it meant, being cooped up while others swam and had fun and were free to do whatever came into their minds.

One day in the mail he received an invitation to the twins' overnight birthday party. He had a whole week to think about it before he was supposed to call and accept or decline the invitation. All through that week he struggled with himself. He wanted to go and yet was unwilling to admit it, or he didn't want to go and yet thought he should. Finally he picked up the phone. He coughed twice to clear his throat while he listened to the ring.

"I'd like to come to the party," he said very fast, not even having noticed if the person who answered was a woman's voice or one of the twins.

"Who is this?" a woman asked.

"David Earl. I got the invi—"

"What number are you calling?"

"Isn't this 467?"

"No, it isn't, dear. This is 457. Dial again."

He didn't.

He rushed out of the house, feeling humiliated, stupid, and angry at himself, and sat for hours in the dark garage thinking. He was a misfit, he decided. It was too late for him to join the rest of the world. He had even grown too far apart from boys his own age; he had nothing in common with them. He imagined how it would be if he had gotten the right number and had gone. He would mumble if someone spoke to him and he would have nothing to contribute to any of their conversations. What did they talk about, anyway?

Twice that summer Peter Pollock came to his house, once to ask him to go camping and another time to take him fishing, and he made excuses both times. When one of the twins broke a leg the other stopped by David's house to see if he would like to enter a go-cart competition in his brother's place. Again he made an excuse, and after that no one came to see him.

And now he only seemed to have Gypsy as a friend. He would often come to spy on her and the old woman. Seeing them together made him both miserable and happy. Miserable because he still wanted, more than anything else, to own Gypsy, and happy because he saw that she was loved as much as any horse could be loved. And because of that love he both hated and liked the woman.

He did not dare to ride Gypsy now, not while the woman spent so much time in the stable, even slept there at night. Sometimes he would wait, hoping that Sarah would go shopping and he could be alone with Gypsy long enough to ride her. But she hardly ever seemed to go away.

One day, on his way to summer school, he saw her

Ford in front of the post office. He waited until she came out. She was dressed as if she were going somewhere, and to make sure, he came up to her.

"Hello, David," she said, seeing him. "I'm on my way to Burlington, to get Gypsy some things she needs. Why don't you ever come to see us?"

"I'm going to summer school," he said.

"Oh, I'm sorry. But evenings are so long. Couldn't you come riding one day?"

"Thank you," he said quickly, his mind already on what he was going to do that day. "I will one evening."

He biked furiously all the way to Gypsy's stable. He would have hours with her; he would ride her and talk to her and have his sandwich with her. And for at least one morning his life would be beautiful.

Chapter Nine

The presentiment of disaster came upon her suddenly. She had never been away from Gypsy for quite so long. Before leaving for Burlington she decided to leave Gypsy in the stable since it looked as if it might rain. She had been gone for over five hours, and stopping in Cornwall for two boxes of lettuce, she suddenly felt that something was wrong. She scanned the sky for any sign of fire. That was her first thought, that somehow the house or even the stable had caught fire, but the sky looked gray and ominous with rain clouds and no smoke was visible anywhere.

She drove fast, skidding on the turns of the dirt road. She rushed into the stable and immediately saw that her intuition was right. Gypsy was out of her stall, standing over an empty basket which had been filled with corn Sarah had got from Margaret's garden a few days ago. The horse looked heavy, her stomach distended, her big eyes listless. Every ear of corn was gone.

"Oh, Gypsy, I didn't lock the gate!" Sarah wailed, leading the heavy-footed horse into her stall.

She rushed to the house and called Lee Earl.

"Gypsy has gotten into some corn," she cried out, tears streaming down her face. "She looks very sick."

"How many ears did she eat?"

"Three dozen."

"That's bad. She'll probably get colic unless you walk her. Just keep walking her. Don't give her any water to drink, just keep walking her. If she wants to lie down, and she probably will, don't let her! Kick her, hit her, but don't let her lie down. Once she lies down she's as good as dead. Horses can't fight, or don't want to fight, for their lives. They'll just lie and wait for death. Don't let her lie down. Keep walking her."

"Will you come over?"

"I can't now. I must go and shoe some horses which have to be shipped to a show tomorrow. But Gypsy'll be all right if you walk her, and I'll come as soon as I can."

"Shouldn't I call the vet?"

"The vet won't walk her for you and that's the best remedy. If she looks like she wants to lie down, put a rope around her neck and pull her up. I've heard of horses getting into twice that much corn and coming through."

Sarah rushed back into the stable, praying that she would not find Gypsy already lying down. Gypsy was standing, but the look on her face told Sarah how ill she felt. Putting a halter on her, Sarah took Gypsy out and began to walk her.

"Oh, my darling," Sarah was saying, tears running now uncontrollably from her eyes. "I couldn't bear it if anything were to happen to you. Why is it that I didn't check that gate? What made me forget? And why did you have to eat all that corn? Corn is bad for you—I knew that—but it was to be a treat, an ear at a time. No, keep your head up, and keep on walking, my love."

The rain came slowly, the drops small and falling far apart. But the sky darkened and it started to rain in earnest. In Burlington she had looked for a rain blanket for Gypsy but couldn't find one. She got out an old horse blanket that Father Connen had talked someone into giving him, and put it on top of Gypsy to keep her dry. She herself was soon soaked to the skin, and she shivered as she continued talking to her horse.

"We're not young anymore, you and I. But the

time hasn't come for either one of us to die. We'll see a winter together, we'll keep warm together, and then, together, we'll welcome spring. . . . I don't blame you for eating that corn. I blame myself. Don't think I'm mad at you. I could never be angry at you. I should never leave you, not even for a little while."

Before Lee left to shoe the show horses, he told David what had happened to Gypsy. The boy waited until his father's truck pulled out of the driveway before getting on his bicycle and starting off for the old woman's house. The rain caught him halfway. He had wanted to admit to the woman that it had been his fault, that it was he who had left the stall gate open, but the closer he got to her house the harder it became to confess this. If he did, he would have to admit to sneaking into the stable, to riding Gypsy in secret. He would have to admit to spying on the two of them. He was ashamed now of the secretiveness of his actions and especially ashamed to confront the woman.

Huddled against the rain next to the wall of the stable, afraid to move, afraid of what he had done, hating himself for his cowardice, he heard each word the woman said to her horse. He knew he should come out, help the woman, take over walking Gypsy. Yet he could not move, and he despised himself for the strength of his fear.

The dark of night came earlier, with the sun hidden by layers of thick, black clouds. They continued walking in the enclosure of the pasture. The rain fell steadily. It was ten o'clock before Sarah gave up. She could not take another step. Her arms were so weary from holding Gypsy's head up that they were numb with pain; her knees were buckling under her. She brought Gypsy into the stable, lit the kerosene lamp, took off the soaking-wet blanket, and rushed into the house to call the veterinarian.

David had only a few moments alone with Gypsy. He was crying as he tried to rub her dry with feed bags, not able to say anything to the horse, for in the soft light of the lamp she looked very ill, and her appearance filled him with dread.

He heard the woman's footsteps on the gravel outside and barely had time to duck behind the rocking chair.

"He is on his way, darling," Sarah said to Gypsy, stroking her. "The doctor will be here soon. I'll sit right here beside you, but you, you must keep on standing. We won't walk anymore. You need a rest too. It's so dark and wet outside."

She shivered, and David could see that her clothes were completely soaked. To keep from falling asleep the woman talked to her horse, and the more she talked the more ashamed David felt of listening, for it seemed to him that he was overhearing private words of love. And before the doctor arrived, David's shame turned into a lashing self-hatred.

"Walking her," the veterinarian said to the woman,

"saved her from colic. She'll be all right after I give her a shot, an enema, and some medicine. You better go in and change your clothes, and if you have some whiskey in the house, take a slug. I'll attend to everything here."

David watched the doctor from his hiding place and did not think much of the way he worked. He knew a bad vet from a good one by the way they approached the animals more than by anything else. This one was obviously afraid. He wanted to shout to him that Gypsy was a very gentle mare, the gentlest horse in the world, but he did not. When the vet took out the large needle and syringe, David looked away. He couldn't bear to watch as the vet gave Gypsy a shot in the neck.

When Sarah came back in dry clothes, he was finished.

"You have a well-behaved horse. Had I known that, I would have given her her shot in the hindquarters rather than in the neck."

"Will she be all right?"

"Yes, she'll be all right now. Call me in the morning, anyway, and tell me how she spent the night." He reached into the bag and brought out a bottle. "There is enough here for five doses. I'll give her some now, and you give her some later tonight and twice tomorrow morning, at eight and ten."

He showed her how to force the bottle into

Gypsy's mouth behind her teeth and pour the medicine down her throat.

"Is it all right if she lies down now?"

"Yes, she won't get colic anymore."

A few minutes after the veterinarian left, Lee Earl drove in. "I saw the doc on the road," he said, looking at Gypsy and smiling at her woeful expression. "He said you'll be all right, you greedy mare."

"But she still looks so sick," the woman said, grateful for his presence.

"Well, she got herself into a mess of trouble, that's why she looks this way. But she'll be fine. You leave her alone now and make yourself some hot coffee."

"Will you have some?"

"Sure, but I bet you haven't had any dinner. I brought you a ham sandwich."

Tears came again to Sarah's eyes, this time tears of gratitude and relief. Suddenly she was sure that her horse was going to be all right.

As soon as Sarah and Lee left the stable, David walked over to Gypsy and put his arms around her neck and stood for a long while not speaking, not crying anymore.

He did not know why, but suddenly he felt himself at peace with the world. Maybe, he thought, it was because Gypsy was going to be all right now. Maybe that's why he felt as though everything else would be all right.

"One day," he whispered to Gypsy, "I'll make it up to you. I promise I will. I don't know how yet, but I'll make it up to you and to her." He waited until his father's car pulled away before getting on his bike and pedaling furiously toward home.

Sarah went to the stable to spend the night. Lee had assured her that there was nothing to be worried about anymore. Gypsy had been given only a carton of lettuce leaves, and she had barely touched them. The medicine must have tasted very bad, for she kept making faces long after swallowing it.

"Lee was telling me," Sarah said to her horse, "about getting some horses ready for a show. I didn't tell him, but I would so like to take you out into the world. I'd like to take you to a horse show. You are the most beautiful of all the horses who ever lived, and I'm sure the judges would know it." She laughed. "Oh, but you must have been in many horse shows in your life! You must have won many ribbons, and maybe you were even a great champion! How I wish I knew something about your past!"

Throughout that night Sarah would fall asleep for a few minutes and wake up and see that Gypsy was standing up and not lying down as was her custom. By the time the dawn came, Sarah noticed that Gypsy's neck had become very stiff. She no longer moved it up and down to search for food or to either side of her. Something is wrong, terribly wrong, she thought, frightened. As she led Gypsy out of the stable, the horse swayed weakly on her legs. Outside, although her eyes looked hungrily toward the green of grass, Gypsy would not lower her head. Sarah handed her a few handfuls of grass, then left her standing in front of the house while she went to call Dr. King.

"Her neck is stiff, and so are her legs! What should I do? She looks as sick today as she did last night."

"I gave her a shot in the neck. That's why it's stiff, but the stiffness will go away in a day or two," he told her. "And she is weak on her legs because she was a pretty sick horse. Give her time to recuperate."

"But she can't reach the grass!" Sarah almost shouted. She was angry at the man. Why had he sent her away to change her clothes? Why had he given Gypsy a shot in the neck instead of the flank? The needle might have damaged a muscle.

"I can't help you there," he said. "As I said, the stiffness will go away. If you want anything else, don't hesitate to call me."

She was furious at his indifference and let the receiver bang down. She walked her horse slowly toward a hill, muttering to herself about the inefficiency of veterinarians. She made Gypsy stand on the flat area of the ground and placed her stiff neck toward the steep slope. That way Gypsy grazed for a while, moving around the hill. All through the day

Sarah nursed her horse. She gave her a hot liniment bath, then massaged Gypsy's legs gently. She held the hay and feed up for Gypsy to reach, watering her the same way. She walked her around slowly on a lead line; she brushed off the flies and stayed with her all that day long, never leaving her, not even to eat herself. Toward evening Lee came and made her rest and eat while he stayed in the stable with Gypsy, rubbing her legs and her neck.

Unable to stay away from her horse, Sarah was back within minutes.

"How is David these days?" she asked.

"He's got a bad cold today after being out last night in the rain. He wasn't home when I got back, and when he did come in he was soaking wet. He told me he had played hooky from summer school. And for a while last night we talked to each other. Almost the way we used to."

Sarah nodded absentmindedly. She could not concentrate on anything but Gypsy.

The next day Gypsy was much better, although still weak. The stiffness of her neck was not as pronounced, and toward evening she could reach the grass and hay, but did so gingerly.

"We'll wait until spring," Sarah told Gypsy that night. "In the spring there is a big western horse show in Burlington, and nothing on this earth is going to prevent us from going. In the spring both of us will go out and show the world that you deserve the biggest, the brightest, and most beautiful ribbon. And we'll hang it in a frame, right over your feeder."

Chapter Ten

She was in the stable giving Gypsy her breakfast when she heard the hoofbeats. Gypsy heard them first, for she raised her head away from the oats and her ears folded back against her neck.

"We have company," Sarah said. "Thank goodness I've already brushed you and you look beautiful."

Gypsy snorted. Sarah could see that she was nervously excited. Her oats went unfinished; the hoofbeats getting closer made her turn completely away from her feed now. She stood, her nostrils wide, her tail high, her head next to Sarah's, looking out of the stable door toward the road.

"It's Margaret Evans and Father Connen! And look at the beautiful horses they're riding!"

Gypsy scraped the floor with her hoof and shivered slightly.

"You are excited, aren't you? Oh, Gypsy, you poor darling, you haven't seen a fellow horse since you've been with me."

"Happy birthday!" Father Connen and Margaret Evans shouted as they drew near.

She had completely forgotten about her own birthday, and was very surprised and pleased that they had remembered.

"We hired these horses so that we could take you two on a pack trip," Margaret announced, getting off her gray and white gelding. "This was going to be a surprise for you, but judging from Gypsy's face, the surprise is on her."

Gypsy, her neck extended out of the stable door, did indeed look terribly surprised, and they all laughed.

"We brought lunch for three," Father Connen said, "and this bag you see on the back of my palomino is full of hay, just in case our mounts run out of grass."

"So get ready, you two females," Margaret commanded.

When they set off, it was Gypsy who insisted on leading the way, her feet prancing, her head turning back to see that the two geldings were following her.

"I do believe," Margaret said, laughing, "that this mare of yours thinks the whole world revolves around her."

"Well, doesn't it?" Sarah said.

Fall had come suddenly that year, turning the leaves overnight into a splendid riot of outrageous colors. They rode under the sapphire of a cloudless sky, surrounded by the loveliness of the land and the warmth of the day. They trespassed merrily over the fields that were turning golden, through forests that echoed with the crushing of twigs and dry leaves. They rode around a lake and came across six geese noisily guarding some young. The geese fluttered their great wings angrily, and the horses waited patiently for the birds to take to the water.

On a great open field, Father Connen suggested they play a game of hat snatching on horseback. He produced three paper hats and explained that the point of the game was to try to reach for and take off the hat from the other person's head. The one who remained wearing his own hat and those of the other two was to be the winner.

Amidst laughter and the snorting of the pursued and pursuing horses, Father Connen won easily. But at another game, the game of tag, it was Sarah who won twice, Margaret once, and Father Connen not at all.

They ate a picnic of sandwiches that tasted better

than any sandwiches they had ever had. From amidst the hay, Father Connen pulled out a bottle of French wine, and over cupcakes with candles they toasted Sarah and Gypsy. The three horses grazed peacefully, not paying any attention to the picnickers or to one another.

Sarah discovered the fun there was in riding with others. After lunch they galloped, three abreast, as though they were Indians attacking a cavalry outpost. And so the day passed in carefree play, the priest and the two women feeling as if youth itself could be recaptured.

The sun was setting in red flames jaggedly invading the deep blue of the sky when they turned back, singing at the top of their voices and purposely off key in remembrance of the church choir that no longer existed.

With the coming of fall Gypsy began to play a game of her own with her mistress. She would hide from her among the leaves that had turned the red copper of her body. It was only by the white of her face that Sarah would now spot her among the foliage.

"I could swear," Sarah would say, "that you were in the war—not in the cavalry, mind you, but in the infantry. You were probably teaching the soldiers how to camouflage themselves. But you mustn't frighten me so! I've been looking for you for an hour. I thought you'd run away. But you wouldn't, would you? You'd never leave me any more than I would leave you."

Chapter Eleven

After the incident with the corn, David did not stop spying on the woman and her horse. He was drawn to them as if they inhabited a magnetic field. Every moment he could spare from his studies, he would ride his bicycle over and stand hiding behind some bush or outside the stable window. He had seen the woman's awkward love for her animal develop into an easy, deep, and endless affection. They had become so used to each other, the woman and Gypsy, that they seemed to David extensions of each other, as if one could no longer exist without the other. There was no more jealousy in him. Rather, he was filled with a wistful feeling of being part of them, and the peacefulness of their relationship filled him with peace. Yet he knew he was living a borrowed life.

His own life, at home and at school, seemed to him quite gray. Although he was closer to his father again, he could not recapture the friendship that once had been his whole life. His father, having ceased to be his hero, was merely a parent. David knew that they both needed each other, but there were other, more obscure, needs that left him with a melancholy feeling of unfulfillment. Sometimes during the day, but most often at night, he felt his loneliness so acutely that it seemed like physical pain.

When he was able to ride Gypsy, always in secret and always afraid of being discovered, he was most keenly aware of that aloneness.

"You don't feel sorry for yourself, do you?" he would whisper into the horse's ear. "I mean, you don't feel sorry for yourself just because you have no one to talk to? The thing is I probably would hate it, to have someone around all the time, bugging me with questions and things. It's probably just as well not to have friends and things. If you don't have anything much, then you can't lose anything, isn't that right?"

There was no answer to his question. But it was Gypsy and only her he could talk to. She alone had taken the place of his father, the place of friends. Often on nights when the woman would be asleep in her house, he would not even ride Gypsy but would sit on her straw, or the rocking chair, talking to her.

But on nights he did ride her, there was no need for talk. They both enjoyed those excursions into the dew-covered, darkened world. He took good care of Gypsy, not letting her run more than she should, and walking her along the grassy bank of the highway before bringing her into the stable. He always made sure that she was dry and would rub her chest with feed bags.

One night, when the moon was full, David decided to try Gypsy out with a lasso. He was going to work from the saddle. It was one of those brisk autumn nights, with frost in the air, a clear night that foreboded the coming of cold weather. The boy and the horse had wandered off quite far, and finding the flat stretch of a field, had practiced barrel turns and then roping. David had discovered that Gypsy knew very well how to act when a rope is thrown. As he threw the lasso, the other end of the rope being tied to the saddle horn, she would come to an immediate stop, even before he jumped down. Rushing to where the loop lay on the ground, he would pretend to be a calf, struggling against Gypsy's pull. And Gypsy would steadily back up until the tugging stopped. Then she would stand waiting for her reward, a pat on the neck. That night, as they were coming back, David was a little worried. The field on which they had played was cut by a stream, and Gypsy's feet had gotten wet. He had nothing with which to dry them, and he realized that the cool breeze and frosty air could make her founder. Once back in the stable, he rubbed her feet, but the damage, if there was any damage, had been done.

Next evening when he was eating dinner with his father, the telephone rang.

"It might be for you," his father said.

"Nobody'd call me," David said.

"Oh, hello, Mrs. Tierney," he heard his father say. David had been praying she would not call. Her call could only mean one thing—Gypsy had foundered. "When did you notice it? . . . It might be a stone. Did you look at her hoofs? Yes . . . How stiff does she seem to you?"

It did happen! Gypsy did founder! And it was his fault!

"I'll come right over," his father said and hung up.

"Can I go with you?"

His father looked surprised and then pleased. "Sure," he said.

What will I do, David thought, what will I do if I have ruined Gypsy forever? Once during the first year of his travels with his father, a roper he knew foundered his horse, and rather than see it in pain, he shot the animal. David had not known what was about to take place as he stood and listened to the men, as he watched the roper pull a gun and fire into the horse's ear. He did not know what had happened even after the horse fell down. And when he did realize that what he had seen was death, violent and unjust death, he had been sick.

"She will be blaming herself," his father was saying. "Mrs. Tierney will think that she has hurt Gypsy if she has foundered. . . ."

"It wasn't her fault." David had spoken before realizing what he was saying.

"No, we mustn't make her think it's her fault. It can happen anytime, even with the best of care."

His father had not guessed what he had started to say.

"What did she say on the phone?" David asked calmly.

"That Gypsy seems to have difficulty walking. She noticed it this morning and thought that she was just stiff, but this evening, when she was riding her, she decided something was really wrong."

"Do you think she's foundered?"

"Sounds like it to me."

He should admit his guilt now. And he should also confess that the incident with the corn had been his fault. But he couldn't. He couldn't bring himself to speak to his father.

He looked at the profile of his father's face. The scars seemed to make it a hard, rugged face. When the bull had torn into his father that day when David was eight, and when he saw him getting up, faceless, in a red mask of blood, David had fainted. It was the one and only time in his life that he had done that. And when he came to, the first thing he saw was his father, holding a towel to the side of his face and smiling down at him. Before they took him to the doctor, he had said, "Don't worry. I'm all right." Coming out of that unconsciousness and seeing him there, seeing him swaying on his feet, seeing him and not some stranger, was the beginning of David's pride in his father. The pride enveloped his love for him, as if love needed to be protected, as if love alone were not enough. A wave of that old love swept over David now, and he turned his face away toward the window because he felt hot tears in his eyes and he certainly didn't want his father to notice that he was crying.

She was waiting for them in the stable. It was the first time David noticed that the woman looked tired and old. It was the same look of tiredness he used to see on the faces of the older men who competed in rodeos, the ones who never won any purses, the ones who got hurt when falling from a bucking bronco, the ones whose hands shook as they worked the ropes. They were the old-timers, maybe good once but now robbed by age of their abilities. They wore a perpetually tired expression, and he always hoped that expression meant, "I know I am old and I know I am tired, but I want to try once more." He did not want to pity them, and he did not want anyone else to pity them. There was something fiercely possessive about that, about his desire to protect them from pity. And now seeing the woman's tired face, the worried look, the softness of her, the vulnerability of her age, he felt a surge of compassion. He wanted to throw himself in the path of any misfortune that might befall her or her horse.

His father was in the stall examining Gypsy's feet, then taking her out, talking to her gently, stroking her neck. He walked her by the light of the head-lights, holding her by the lead line, watching her every step, seeing what David was seeing, a stiff-kneed walk, a stumbling movement of her front legs. There was no doubt in David's mind that the horse had foundered. He waited breathlessly for his father to confirm this.

"What do you think?" The woman's voice was no more than a whisper, yet to David it seemed that she had cried the question out loudly.

"It's hard to tell," Lee said, leading Gypsy back into her stall. "I had hoped that only one leg was affected, but it looks like both are. And that could mean founder."

"What's that?"

David looked away from the woman's expression of fear.

"I don't say it is, mind you." Lee smiled encouragingly.

"But what is it and how could she have gotten it?"

117

"Blood gets coagulated in the legs. And most horses founder for one of three reasons: they haven't been properly cooled off after being ridden, or they have been given too much water or food too soon after being ridden, or they have gotten chilled, especially if they stood in cold wind or water after a long ride."

"But I've tried to be so careful about her," Sarah said, and then, approaching her horse, she put both arms around its neck and buried her face in Gypsy's mane. She turned sharply to Lee. "Is she in pain?"

"Oh, yes, she's in pain if she has laminitis."

"Laminitis?"

"That's founder. But she might not—"

"How can I find out?"

"We can call Doc King."

"Oh, no, not him! I couldn't ever trust him. Isn't there anyone else? Isn't there a good vet anywhere around?"

"There is a fine one in Burlington."

"I'll take her there."

"We'll have to rent a horse trailer."

"We'll rent one."

"He'll take an X-ray."

"And then we'll be sure?"

"Yes, then we'll be sure."

"And—" she hesitated, her eyes very large, frightened now—"if it's bad. Then what?"

"It won't be bad," Lee said firmly. "Gypsy's a

healthy mare. It might be a number of things. Sprains or fever or a pulled tendon."

"Will you come with me to Burlington?"

"Of course. You'll need my truck to hitch the trailer to."

"Tomorrow? Can you make it tomorrow?"

"Sure," he said. "I'll be here with a trailer a little after four."

David heard their words as if from a long distance. He had decided to run away. It was the only thing for him to do. He was no longer fit to live among people. He had become like some sort of disease, inflicting pain on the people around him. He would run away and live in the forest, like a wild animal. And his punishment would be not knowing what happened to Gypsy. His punishment would be wondering, as long as he lived, whether she got well or whether she had to be destroyed. And if the latter was to happen, it would also be the end of the old woman. She would most certainly die from grief.

It was after nine thirty when they got back to the house.

"Will you come with us tomorrow?" his father asked.

"I don't know if I can," David answered, not looking at him. "It depends on how much homework I have."

"The homework could wait for once!"

"Then maybe I'll come along," David said and then added quickly, because he was afraid he'd start crying, "I'd better turn in now. Good night, Dad." He had not called him Dad since they had moved to Vermont. And, he thought, he would never get to call him that again.

David decided to leave a note. When he tried running away before, he was going in anger. Now he was going because he didn't want to keep on hurting his father. But he could not say that in a letter. He stared at the blank piece of paper in desperation. Finally he began to write.

> *Dear Dad,*
> *I am sorry about everything. I'm the one responsible for Gypsy foundering. And the time she got into the corn was my fault too. I don't even have enough guts to tell Mrs. Tierney that myself. I wish you'd do it for me. I hope I have not killed her horse! I'm sorry about this last year, about how mean I've been to you. Maybe before I die I'll do something worthwhile to make you proud, but I doubt that I will. Please don't look for me this time. I must go away because I'm not fit to live with people.*
>
> > *Good-bye, Dad.*

When he signed his name, he reread the letter. He had not told his father that he still loved him, like before, but maybe, he thought, he'd guess that. He lay on the bed waiting for his father's footsteps. He would not leave until his father had gone to bed. He almost fell asleep waiting, and this made him mad at himself. How could he ever be able to sleep after what he had done? Only people with clear consciences should be able to sleep. He got up and threw sweaters and two shirts and a pair of socks into his book bag. He put on his leather jacket and waited five minutes after hearing his father close his bedroom door. He carried his shoes in his hand, walking down the stairs.

He took his bike. The bike would help him get farther away. Still he didn't know where it was that he was going. Toward the mountains, he decided. But that would mean passing Mrs. Tierney's property. He pedaled fast, trying not to think of all the other times he had hurried down the highway toward Gypsy. It was just before reaching the woman's driveway that he changed his mind. He would go and see her. He owed her that much. He owed her admission of his guilt. Otherwise she would go on blaming herself. He didn't want her to do that, not even for another hour.

There was a light in the stable, but the house was dark. He opened the door. She was asleep in her rocking chair, and Gypsy was lying down in her stall. He watched them both for a moment, the old woman, a black shawl around her shoulders, looked very fragile, very small. And the horse, having lifted its head, had put it down again and closed its eyes. There was so much beauty in her big brown body extended on the straw, the legs drawn in, the hips round and smooth, shining by the light of the oil lamp. David swallowed hard, approached the woman, and touched her shoulder gently. She opened her eyes immediately.

"Oh," she sighed. "I was just dreaming about you, David." She smiled. "You'll never believe it, but this is the very first time I've ever remembered a dream. We were riding together and—" She suddenly straightened up and a worried look replaced the smile. "But David, what are you doing here at this hour?"

"I came to tell you." He shivered involuntarily and spoke very fast. "I'm going away and I wanted you to know that it was my fault. I took Gypsy out riding last night. She got her feet wet and that's why she foundered." A tremendous sense of relief suddenly came over him. And oddly enough Mrs. Tierney was looking at him kindly. "And the other time," he continued, more loudly now, "the time she got into the corn, I had been riding her that day too. And I forgot to close her gate."

He waited for her to say something but she didn't.

"And that's why"—he raised his voice, almost shouting now—"I'm running away."

"You're not doing anything of the sort," she said quickly, a little angrily. "You're staying right here. You're going to do everything possible to make Gypsy well again. That's what you're going to do."

"But—"

"David!" She reached both hands out to him. "David, don't you see? It's all right now. You told me, and in telling me you punished yourself. I am very glad that you have been riding Gypsy."

"You are?"

"But of course I am. I asked you to. You know, I've always felt that she is your horse as much as she's mine. She was meant to be yours. Your father wanted to buy her for you."

She stopped speaking and began to smile at David.

"You know, David," she said very quietly, "I thought I was the luckiest person in the world, having found Gypsy. But you are even luckier than I. You are needed more than I. Your father needs you. And now both Gypsy and I need you too."

He knelt beside her chair and she hugged him then, and while she held him there came over him a feeling of absolute peace. He clung to her and felt safe and saved, as if some awful danger had been removed, as if nothing could ever go terribly wrong again.

"We will make her well," he said. "I just know we will. We'll soak her feet and rub her and walk her and do everything—"

"And you'll come to the doctor tomorrow?"

"Of course I'll come with you."

And then Gypsy got to her feet and yawned. They both laughed, watching as she yawned again and again, her large face seeming to laugh too as the yawn stretched her mouth wide.

It was well after midnight when David came home. Sarah had driven him back.

"You know," David said to her as he was getting out of the car, "you're right about being lucky when people need you. And I know he"—David nodded his head toward the house—"can use me around the house. And you and Gypsy, you'll need me too."

"Yes, David, all three of us depend on you."

"Thanks," he said, and then impulsively he leaned across the seat and kissed her on the cheek.

The feeling of happiness made David hungry, and he went into the kitchen for a sandwich and a glass of milk. His father was seated at the kitchen table holding David's letter in his hands. He looked up at David, and for a moment his eyes were cloudy. They looked at each other, not saying anything, and both felt the unbearably wonderful mixture of happiness and peace. And then his father got up and went to the icebox.

"What will you have?" he asked David.

"Gee, Dad, I think I'd like a sandwich made of everything that's in there."

Chapter Twelve

C Ω "What if—" David asked his father as they approached the woman's house, "what if Doc Smith says it's founder?"

"If it is," his father replied slowly, "I don't think Mrs. Tierney will be able to bear to see Gypsy suffer. The first time she hears Gypsy groan, and sees her sweat and refuse to get up—"

"She hasn't foundered!" David shouted then, not wanting his father to go on.

They were waiting, Gypsy wearing her blanket and the woman a warm coat in which she seemed to shiver.

"Can I ride in the trailer?" she wanted to know.

"It's too small," Lee said.

Into the built-in feeder Sarah put some hay and grains and a few handfuls of lettuce leaves. They had no trouble getting Gypsy into the trailer, but her legs seemed very weak and her walk stiff-kneed. They didn't talk much on the way to Burlington, but just before turning into Dr. Smith's driveway Sarah said, "I've read about laminitis in the *Horseman's Encyclopedia*. It didn't say that it's incurable, but it did say about the pain. Do they recover?"

"Sometimes," Lee said.

"I think," Sarah said quietly, "that it might be better if she didn't have to suffer."

Dr. Smith, a giant of a man, watched as Gypsy backed out of the trailer and walked toward the stable.

"She walks so much better!" Sarah whispered in awe. And indeed Gypsy's walk, although not perfect, was remarkably improved.

"That often happens," Dr. Smith said, his eyes on the horse as it was being led around by Lee. "When they brace themselves in the trailer they're using muscles that they didn't even know they had."

"Then it's not founder!" Sarah exclaimed.

"Why does every horse owner," Dr. Smith asked no one in particular, "always think the animal's foundered? To me this looks as if she's pulled a tendon on her right foot and has been favoring the other. Did you bring the bridle with you?"

"No," David said, "but if you want me to trot her on the pavement, I could do it without one."

"You know a lot about horses, don't you?" Dr. Smith said, smiling as David hoisted himself on Gypsy's back. "That's the very best way to check on a pulled tendon, by trotting the animal on hard pavement."

Gypsy didn't have to trot far for the doctor to confirm his diagnosis.

"You'll be all right!" Sarah was saying loudly, hugging Gypsy, burying her face in the horse's neck.

"It could have happened anytime, couldn't it?" David was asking the doctor.

"Sure. She could even have pulled it getting up in the stall or walking in the pasture. It can happen sometimes when they shift weight while they're standing still. Of course," he looked at David and smiled, "if you've been riding her over very rough terrain, it could be your fault."

"But she'll be all right, won't she?" Sarah was asking.

"She'll be all right," the doctor answered, "only if you take good care of her. I'll give her a shot of cortisone. Lee will pull off her shoes, and she'll need plenty of rest, some walking on a lead line and daily soaking of her right foot in Epsom salts. Later on she might need special heeled shoes, but maybe she'll recover so completely that that won't be necessary.

She shouldn't be ridden, of course, and by Christmas she should be as good as new." He pried open Gypsy's mouth. "She's sixteen, and by spring she could be in good enough shape to be in foal again."

The cure began that very same day. Lee devised a plastic stocking which kept the hot compresses warm. David managed to find a battery-powered massager which helped the circulation of the blood in Gypsy's legs. Now each day after school David would bicycle over to Sarah's house. Together they would attend to Gypsy. They would baby her as if the very fact that she had not foundered was something that they had to reward with constant care and abounding love. Their common attention to the horse drew them close together, and neither one could any longer imagine life without the other.

"Just a short while ago," David told Sarah one day, "I didn't care about the future or anything much. But now I know what it is that I want to do with my life. I'll study to be a vet. But that's not the important part. Do you want to guess what the most important thing in my life is going to be?"

"It has something to do with horses, doesn't it?"

"Yes, but you'd never guess!" His eyes were bright on her. "I want to have a sort of nursing home for old horses. You know, a place where the very old ones, the ones that can no longer be ridden, or work, or anything, can come to rest. I want to give them a good time before they die. I will go to auctions and find those that should no longer be used, and I'll buy them and bring them to this place I'll have, a farmlike place, with great big pastures, lots of shade and water. They will have the best of care, because I'll be a vet then, and lots of company and good food, and no one will be riding them or working them. They will just lead lazy lives and be so spoiled that if they were ever abused they will no longer remember. And I'll even advertise, in all sorts of newspapers and magazines, that I'll take old horses and keep them for nothing so that even people who are good to their animals but don't know what to do with them when they grow old can send me theirs. And it won't be a sad place. It will be big and the horses will feel free, and they will graze over acres of green grass and there will be no one asking them to do anything."

Even before he stopped talking she knew he need not wait to grow up. She could make his dream a reality.

"Oh, David!" she shouted, hugging him. "This farm, wouldn't it make a perfect place? The barn is there. It used to house forty cows once. If we make box stalls, we could have twenty horses there, at least, and there are streams running through the fields and plenty of trees for shade. All we'd need do would be to fence the whole thing in. Isn't it perfect?"

They were laughing and making their plans when

Lee drove in to pick up David. When they told him what they were planning to do he was immediately carried away by the idea.

"It wouldn't take hardly any work at all," he said. "We could hire a few of the boys from your school to help us with the fencing—"

"There're the twins, and Peter Pollock," David interrupted. "I know they'd help us—"

"And the barn," Lee went on, "it's in great shape except it would need a wooden floor and partitions, but I know of a place where I can pick up the lumber, used planks, for next to nothing, and there is also an old house that they wanted to burn down, and I can get the flooring off that."

"We'll start in the spring," Sarah said and laughed. "By the summer, by the beginning of summer we will have our first horse, and Gypsy will have company."

"She won't ever be jealous," David assured her, "because her stable will always be her very own, and the others will realize she's a queen here."

That evening when David and his father had gone back to their own house, Sarah sat down to write her will. She left her property and all her money, her husband's insurance and her own, as well as her small income, to Lee in trust for David, to be used for what she called "a horse kingdom." And that night she dreamt again, and remembered the dream when she woke up. She had dreamt of horses, old, misused horses, acres of them, feeding on grass, sunbathing, nuzzling each other, moving slowly, some running, others standing still, as if lost in dreams; and among them stood Gypsy with a foal by her side.

Chapter Thirteen

Before the first snows fell, Gypsy was over her pulled tendon. For her, life had not changed. She was now cared for as much by David as by Sarah; her daily massages continued; she was ridden by both, the boy and the woman, and both of them spoiled her and let her run whenever she wanted to, but not quite as much as before.

But for the people who loved her, nothing seemed quite the same. Lee was planning to sell his house and use the money from it for all the necessary things which would turn Sarah Tierney's farm into a shelter for old horses. She had invited him and David to come and live with her as soon as their house was sold.

"It doesn't make any sense for me to live alone in this big house," she told them. "And besides you'll be here all the time getting things ready, and once the horses arrive, we'll have much to do, so we'll hire a woman to do the housework and cooking, and the three of us will spend all our time with the horses."

When the weather turned cold, Sarah asked Lee to come and install a potbellied stove in the stable.

"But horses don't feel the cold as bad as people," he told her. "Besides, they grow winter coats."

"A Vermont winter is too awful even for a horse," she insisted, and the stove was put in. She banked it at night and the fire never went out. It was an additional chore, carrying the coal and keeping the fire going, but she did it with love, as she did everything that concerned her horse. Besides, she now had David, who did a hundred helpful little things without ever being asked.

In the early afternoons before David would come, she would sit in her rocking chair next to the stove, and she would take her afternoon naps. And now each time she fell asleep she would dream, each dream celebrating something new in her horse. She dreamt of Gypsy as a movie horse, pursuing the bad men under the hot California sun; she dreamt of her as the winner of important horse shows; she dreamt of her always as a fearless and noble animal, a legendary horse, a creature so splendid that her life and exploits extended from biblical times through the most important events in man's history to the present day. And each time she dreamt, she would remember the dream clearly and tell it to Gypsy and to David.

The first snow, when it fell hesitantly, did not please Gypsy. She walked around, forlornly hunting for her grass; and finding it gone, she began to dig for it with her nose, helping herself with a hoof. Giving her her daily exercise or watching David ride her, Sarah would worry about the horse's hoofs, which would pack snow until they formed white balls. She would dismount often and pick the hoofs clean, and David would do the same. But when the next snow fell, four inches of light powder followed by a sun-filled day, she rode Gypsy as if through a sea, the white spray coming high from the horse's running legs. And coming back, she found David waiting for them in the stable to help her rub Gypsy dry. He was always there, each afternoon now, and sometimes he would bring the twins or Peter with him. She would help them with their homework, delighted to discover that eighth-grade arithmetic was not beyond her.

When the weather deteriorated and the cold gripped everything in an unmerciful freeze, Sarah could not bear to have Gypsy stay in a stable that could no longer be made warm even with a red-hot stove. During the coldest nights she would bring Gypsy into the kitchen of the house. With David's help she folded the large table and made a sort of stall, with newspapers on the floor and a thick covering of straw for Gypsy's bed.

"You know," she explained to her horse, "this is as much for me as it is for you. Your house was getting much too cold for my old bones. And besides, it was too cold for our guest, for David. I hated to see his nose get so red."

She was somewhat ashamed of having moved Gypsy into the house, but when Father Connen and Margaret Evans came to see her on separate visits, they, together with Lee, agreed that there was nothing terribly strange in a horse living in the kitchen.

"If it were any other horse," Margaret said, "it would look crazy, but Gypsy seems to belong here just as much as you, Sarah."

One day before Christmas Lee asked David if he'd like a horse as a present.

"No, Dad," David said, "I really wouldn't. Gypsy has always been my horse, in a way, and pretty soon we'll have all those others. If I had a horse of my own then, it wouldn't seem fair. I want to love the old ones, and I don't care if I ever even ride, which sounds crazy even to me." He laughed. "To tell you the truth, Dad, I think I would have made a lousy bronco rider."

That Christmas no one received more presents than Gypsy. She was the center of attention even during Christmas dinner, looking splendid in a new winter blanket and a stone-studded halter.

Sarah didn't know how she caught the cold. The worst of the winter weather was behind them. The snows were thawing and the winds of March were coming from the south. She began to cough, and coughed often, and sometimes it seemed to her that the coughing fit would never end.

Everything she did now took longer. She felt dizzy when she rode Gypsy, and her sore throat made it painful for her to talk to her horse. Cleaning the stable seemed to be a never-ending chore because she would have to stop often to rest. The things she carried became strangely heavy. Sometimes she would have to stop whatever she was doing just to catch the breath that seemed increasingly irregular.

She worried in earnest about the cold not getting better, and for the first time in her life, began to take care of herself, spending the time not with Gypsy but in bed, resting and taking aspirin. She would pretend in front of David that it wasn't a cold at all but spring hay fever. But it was a cold and it did not go away. It became a part of her, with her body weakened by a pain in the chest from the coughing fits.

She had been planning to enter the horse show, but

when Lee came over to see how Gypsy was behaving while being ridden, she knew that she would be too weak to enter it. Still she hoped that Gypsy might go and that David might show her instead.

"I can't believe it," Lee said under his breath as he jumped off Gypsy; and then more loudly, looking at Sarah and then at David, he asked, "How could you two, in such a short time, ruin such a perfectly trained animal?"

"Ruin it?" Sarah asked, her eyes wide with fear. David didn't say anything; he knew what his father meant.

"I mean, spoil it!" Lee sounded disgusted. "Why did you let her get away with everything? I don't blame you, but David ought to know better. If I hadn't been shoeing her I would never believe her to be the same mare you bought only a year ago."

David looked guiltily at the ground, and Gypsy lowered her head also, while Sarah smiled at them.

"I couldn't do a thing with her," Lee continued angrily. "She wouldn't walk for me when I wanted her to walk and she breaks into a lope from a jog. This horse was the best broke critter, and look at her now! You can thank yourself and David and forget all about that horse show unless both of you want to make fools of yourselves."

"I can shape her up," David said suddenly.

"You'd need more than a week," his father said disgustedly, leading Gypsy out of the pasture.

"I can do it in a week," David said quickly. "I can do it in less than that."

"Go ahead. Try it," his father said, "but you'd better work on Mrs. Tierney as much as on Gypsy. As far as I am concerned I have nothing to say about you two, that horse, or the show."

He strode off toward the truck, leaving David to spend the weekend in Sarah's house.

"Your father is very mad—more at me, I think, than at you."

"No, he's mad at me mostly," David said. "He wouldn't have any right to be mad at you. After all, it's your horse and you had a perfect right to spoil her if you wanted to. But I should have been firmer with her. Well, we'd better get to work. I'll just walk her and nothing else, but we'll get her ready for that show yet. I want you to win your first ribbon."

"Would you ride her?" Sarah asked eagerly. "I mean ride her in the show instead of me?"

"No, I wouldn't. Legally it's your horse and you're going to show her."

"But you know how badly I ride and I wouldn't know what to do."

"I'll teach you all about it," he said, jumping on the saddle. "By the time I'm through with both of you, you'll be sick of me and sick of each other."

That day Sarah watched David for more than three hours. She was amazed at his great patience. Gypsy had no intention of walking; she wanted to run.

Fighting the reins, she tossed her neck up and down, raised her feet high, and pranced sideways. Yet David never lost his temper, never stopped talking to her in a gentle, soothing voice. By the time darkness fell Gypsy had quietly walked several times around the pasture. And Sarah had learned by that evening what it means to train a horse. She felt guilty that she had made Gypsy forget what she must have been taught with equal patience once before.

The next day, and throughout the week that followed, David spent all his time preparing Sarah and Gypsy for the show. They worked hard at it, but feeling the horse handle with new ease and intelligence filled Sarah with pride.

While she watched Gypsy and David working she realized that she was often shivering with cold. When she was near David she would hide her flushed cheeks, but it was harder to cover up the cough which now seemed to come from the very depths of her aching body. David was too busy to notice these things, but Gypsy would fold her ears back at the sound of the racking cough that Sarah could no longer muffle with a handkerchief.

She had trouble sleeping at night while the fever rose, and she could tell midnight by its hot peak. She knew that she should spend more time in bed or see a doctor, but she wanted more than anything else to be able to show Gypsy herself.

The morning of the horse show she was too weak to get out of bed. When she heard Lee and David arrive with the trailer, she threw a coat over her nightgown and used all her will power to reach the stable. Her head was burning, and her legs felt as if they were filled with cotton.

"I overslept," she told them. "You'd better start without me. I will catch up."

"You don't look well at all," Lee said.

"I think you have a fever," David said, "you'd better take your temperature."

"I'm all right," she said. "It's just that I slept too long and I'm not used to it."

When Gypsy was in the trailer, Sarah walked in and put her arms around the horse's neck. "It will be David, not I, who'll ride you," she whispered. "You'll have a better chance of winning that ribbon. Be good to him, and miss me, just a bit. And remember that you are going into the world well-loved."

"I don't think we should go," David said when she came out of the trailer. "You ought to go to bed and we should stick around."

"Oh, but you must go, David," Sarah said, and hugged him. "Gypsy is counting so much on bringing back a ribbon. I've promised it to her and we mustn't break that promise. But if I don't get there before the first event, you must ride her. Will you do that, David?"

"Sure, but . . ."

She pushed him gently toward the truck. She had to lean against the stable as she waved good-bye to them. She watched them until they disappeared around the last bend in the road, and then she walked slowly into the stable. Shivering, she stood for a while looking at Gypsy's empty stall. Then she sat down in the rocking chair, wrapping her coat more tightly around herself.

If only she had had a chance to see a horse show. She had no idea what Gypsy would have to do or how hard she would have to compete with other horses. Of course the judges would have to be fair, but, she thought, how could they ever be quite fair to the other horses, once they saw Gypsy?

She closed her eyes and tried to see Gypsy as the people at the horse show would see her. She would not be the tallest of the horses, and certainly not the smallest. Would it be her eyes that would attract them? Or that warm russet glow of her coat? Would they recognize that special softness about her?

Gypsy was standing far away, at the edge of the forest. The copper of her body against the green pines was like a burning fire, her face a patch of white mist. Sarah felt like running toward her horse, but there seemed to be no need to hurry. The distance between them was diminishing fast as she walked across the sunlit meadow, in the deep grass. Her hand was in her husband's hand, and they were walking together toward the horse that stood waiting for them at the edge of the forest.

Author of 19 published books, Maia Wojciechowska won the Newberry Award in 1965 for her young adult novel, *Shadow of a Bull*.

Born in Poland on August 7, 1927, she traveled through war torn Europe as a child and later immigrated to the United States with her family. Her first book, *Market Day for 'Ti André*, was published in 1952, and she didn't attempt another for over ten years. Instead, she tried her hand at being a wife, a mother, a masseuse, an undercover detective, an Avon saleswoman, a ski bum, and a bullfighter. Her unconventional life, which afforded her opportunities to test her own physical and moral courage, inspired her to write novels inhabited by characters who struggle to make brave and inspired choices for themselves.

Before she died in 2002, she raised another child as a single mother, became a grandmother, was an elected councilwoman, was made an honorary member of the Ramapough Indian tribe, and donated her body to medical science.